The Moon Maid

The Moon Maid

by Edgar Rice Burroughs

Contents

Prologue

I MET him in the Blue Room of the Transoceanic Liner Harding the night of Mars Day—June 10, 1967. I had been wandering about the city for several hours prior to the sailing of the flier watching the celebration, dropping in at various places that I might see as much as possible of scenes that doubtless will never again be paralleled—a world gone mad with joy. There was only one vacant chair in the Blue Room and that at a small table at which he was already seated alone. I asked his permission and he graciously invited me to join him, rising as he did so, his face lighting with a smile that compelled my liking from the first.

I had thought that Victory Day, which we had celebrated two months before, could never be eclipsed in point of mad national enthusiasm, but the announcement that had been made this day appeared to have had even a greater effect upon the minds and imaginations of the people.

The more than half-century of war that had continued almost uninterruptedly since 1914 had at last terminated in the absolute domination of the Anglo-Saxon race over all the other races of the World, and practically for the first time since the activities of the human race were preserved for posterity in any enduring form no civilized, or even semi-civilized, nation maintained a battle line upon any portion of the globe. War was at an end—definitely and forever. Arms and ammunition were being dumped into the five oceans; the vast armadas of the air were being scrapped or converted into carriers for purposes of peace and commerce.

The peoples of all nations had celebrated—victors and vanquished alike—for they were tired of war. At least they thought that they were tired of war; but were they? What else did they know? Only the oldest of men could recall even a semblance of world peace, the others knew nothing but war. Men had been born and lived their lives and died with their grandchildren clustered about them—all with the alarms of war ringing constantly in their ears. Perchance the little area of their activities was never actually encroached upon by the iron-shod hoof of battle; but always somewhere war endured, now receding like the salt tide only to return again; until there arose that great tidal wave of human emotion in 1959 that swept the entire world for eight bloody years, and receding, left peace upon a spent and devastated world.

Edgar Rice Burroughs

Two months had passed—two months during which the world appeared to stand still, to mark time, to hold its breath. What now? We have peace, but what shall we do with it? The leaders of thought and of action are trained for but one condition—war. The reaction brought despondency—our nerves, accustomed to the constant stimulus of excitement, cried out against the monotony of peace, and yet no one wanted war again. We did not know what we wanted.

And then came the announcement that I think saved a world from madness, for it directed our minds along a new line to the contemplation of a fact far more engrossing than prosaic wars and equally as stimulating to the imagination and the nerves—intelligible communication had at last been established with Mars!

Generations of wars had done their part to stimulate scientific research to the end that we might kill one another more expeditiously, that we might transport our youth more quickly to their shallow graves in alien soil, that we might transmit more secretly and with greater celerity our orders to slay our fellow men. And always, generation after generation, there had been those few who could detach their minds from the contemplation of massacre and looking forward to a happier era concentrate their talents and their energies upon the utilization of scientific achievement for the betterment of mankind and the rebuilding of civilization.

Among these was that much ridiculed but devoted coterie who had clung tenaciously to the idea that communication could be established with Mars. The hope that had been growing for a hundred years had never been permitted to die, but had been transmitted from teacher to pupil with ever-growing enthusiasm, while the people scoffed as, a hundred years before, we are told, they scoffed at the experimenters with flying machines, as they chose to call them.

About 1940 had come the first reward of long years of toil and hope, following the perfection of an instrument which accurately indicated the direction and distance of the focus of any radio-activity with which it might be attuned. For several years prior to this all the more highly sensitive receiving instruments had recorded a series of three dots and three dashes which began at precise intervals of twenty-four hours and thirty-seven minutes and continued for approximately fifteen minutes. The new instrument indicated conclusively that these signals, if they were signals, originated always at the same distance from the Earth and in the same direction as the point in the universe occupied by the planet Mars.

It was five years later before a sending apparatus was evolved that bade fair to transmit its waves from Earth to Mars. At first their own message was repeated—three dots and three dashes. Although the usual interval of time had not elapsed since we had received their daily signal, ours was immediately answered. Then we sent a message consisting of five dots and two dashes, alternating. Immediately they replied with five dots and two dashes and we knew beyond peradventure of a doubt that we were in communication with the Red Planet, but it required twenty-two years of unremitting effort, with the most brilliant intellects of two worlds concentrated upon it, to evolve and perfect an intelligent system of inter-communication between the two planets.

Today, this tenth of June, 1967, there was published broadcast to the world the first message from Mars. It was dated Helium, Barsoom, and merely extended greetings to a sister world and wished us well. But it was the beginning.

The Blue Room of the Harding was, I presume, but typical of every other gathering place in the civilized world. Men and women were eating, drinking, laughing, singing and talking. The flier was racing through the air at an altitude of little over a thousand feet. Its engines, motivated wirelessly from power plants thousands of miles distant, drove it noiselessly and swiftly along its overnight pathway between Chicago and Paris.

I had of course crossed many times, but this instance was unique because of the epoch-making occasion which the passengers were celebrating, and so I sat at the table longer than usual, watching my fellow diners, with, I imagine, a slightly indulgent smile upon my lips, since—I mention it in no spirit of egotism—it had been my high privilege to assist in the consummation of a hundred years of effort that had borne fruit that day. I looked around at my fellow diners and then back to my table companion.

He was a fine looking chap, lean and bronzed—one need not have noted the Air Corps overseas service uniform, the Admiral's stars and anchors or the wound stripes to have guessed that he was a fighting man; he looked it, every inch of him, and there were a full seventy-two inches.

We talked a little—about the great victory and the message from Mars, of course, and though he often smiled I noticed an occasional shadow of sadness in his eyes and once, after a particularly mad outburst of pandemonium on the part of the celebrators, he shook his head, remarking: "Poor devils!" and then: "It is just as well—let them enjoy life while they may. I envy them their ignorance."

"What do you mean?" I asked.

He flushed a little and then smiled. "Was I speaking aloud?" he asked.

Edgar Rice Burroughs

I repeated what he had said and he looked steadily at me for a long minute before he spoke again. "Oh, what's the use!" he exclaimed, almost petulantly; "you wouldn't understand and of course you wouldn't believe. I do not understand it myself; but I have to believe because I know—I know from personal observation. God! if you could have seen what I have seen."

"Tell me," I begged; but he shook his head dubiously.

"Do you realize that there is no such thing as Time?" he asked suddenly—"That man has invented Time to suit the limitations of his finite mind, just as he has named another thing, that he can neither explain nor understand, Space?"

"I have heard of such a theory," I replied; "but I neither believe nor disbelieve—I simply do not know."

I thought I had him started and so I waited as I have read in fiction stories is the proper way to entice a strange narrative from its possessor. He was looking beyond me and I imagined that the expression of his eyes denoted that he was witnessing again the thrilling scenes of the past. I must have been wrong, though—in fact I was quite sure of it when he next spoke.

"If that girl isn't careful," he said, "the thing will upset and give her a nasty fall—she is much too near the edge."

I turned to see a richly dressed and much dishevelled young lady busily dancing on a table-top while her friends and the surrounding diners cheered her lustily.

My companion arose. "I have enjoyed your company immensely," he said, "and I hope to meet you again. I am going to look for a place to sleep now— they could not give me a stateroom—I don't seem to be able to get enough sleep since they sent me back." He smiled.

"Miss the gas shells and radio bombs, I suppose," I remarked.

"Yes," he replied, "just as a convalescent misses smallpox."

"I have a room with two beds," I said. "At the last minute my secretary was taken ill. I'll be glad to have you share the room with me."

He thanked me and accepted my hospitality for the night—the following morning we would be in Paris.

As we wound our way among the tables filled with laughing, joyous diners, my companion paused beside that at which sat the young woman who had previously attracted his attention. Their eyes met and into hers came a look of puzzlement and half-recognition. He smiled frankly in her face, nodded and passed on.

"You know her, then?" I asked.

"I shall—in two hundred years," was his enigmatical reply.

We found my room, and there we had a bottle of wine and some little cakes and a quiet smoke and became much better acquainted.

It was he who first reverted to the subject of our conversation in the Blue Room.

"I am going to tell you," he said, "what I have never told another; but on the condition that if you retell it you are not to use my name. I have several years of this life ahead of me and I do not care to be pointed out as a lunatic. First let me say that I do not try to explain anything, except that I do not believe prevision to be a proper explanation. I have actually lived the experiences I shall tell you of, and that girl we saw dancing on the table tonight lived them with me; but she does not know it. If you care to, you can keep in mind the theory that there is no such thing as Time—just keep it in mind—you cannot understand it, or at least I cannot. Here goes."

An Adventure in Space

"I HAD intended telling you my story of the days of the twenty-second century, but it seems best, if you are to understand it, to tell first the story of my great-great-grandfather who was born in the year 2000."

I must have looked up at him quizzically, for he smiled and shook his head as one who is puzzled to find an explanation suited to the mental capacity of his auditor.

"My great-great-grandfather was, in reality, the great-great-grandson of my previous incarnation which commenced in 1896. I married in 1916, at the age of twenty. My son Julian was born in 1917. I never saw him. I was killed in France in 1918—on Armistice Day.

"I was again reincarnated in my son's son in 1937. I am thirty years of age. My son was born in 1970—that is the son of my 1937 incarnation —and his son, Julian 5th, in whom I again returned to Earth, in the year 2000. I see you are confused, but please remember my injunction that you are to try to keep in mind the theory that there is no such thing as Time. It is now the year 1967 yet I recall distinctly every event of my life that occurred in four incarnations—the last that I recall being that which had its origin in the year 2100. Whether I actually skipped three generations that time or through some caprice of Fate I am merely unable to visualize an intervening incarnation, I do not know.

"My theory of the matter is that I differ only from my fellows in that I can recall

10

the events of many incarnations, while they can recall none of theirs other than a few important episodes of that particular one they are experiencing; but perhaps I am wrong. It is of no importance. I will tell you the story of Julian 5th who was born in the year 2000, and then, if we have time and you yet are interested, I will tell you of the torments during the harrowing days of the twenty-second century, following the birth of Julian 9th in 2100."

I will try to tell the story in his own words in so far as I can recall them, but for various reasons, not the least of which is that I am lazy, I shall omit superfluous quotation marks—that is, with your permission, of course.

My name is Julian. I am called Julian 5th. I come of an illustrious family —my great-great-grandfather, Julian 1st, a major at twenty-two, was killed in France early in The Great War. My great-grandfather, Julian 2nd, was killed in battle in Turkey in 1938. My grandfather, Julian 3rd, fought continuously from his sixteenth year until peace was declared in his thirtieth year. He died in 1992 and during the last twenty-five years of his life was an Admiral of the Air, being transferred at the close of the war to command of the International Peace Fleet, which patrolled and policed the world. He also was killed in line of duty, as was my father who succeeded him in the service.

At sixteen I graduated from the Air School and was detailed to the International Peace Fleet, being the fifth generation of my line to wear the uniform of my country. That was in 2016, and I recall that it was a matter of pride to me that it rounded out the full century since Julian 1st graduated from West Point, and that during that one hundred years no adult male of my line had ever owned or worn civilian clothes.

Of course there were no more wars, but there still was fighting. We had the pirates of the air to contend with and occasionally some of the uncivilized tribes of Russia, Africa and central Asia required the attention of a punitive expedition. However, life seemed tame and monotonous to us when we read of the heroic deeds of our ancestors from 1914 to 1967, yet none of us wanted war. It had been too well schooled into us that we must not think of war, and the International Peace Fleet so effectively prevented all preparation for war that we all knew there could never be another. There wasn't a firearm in the world other than those with which we were armed, and a few of ancient design that were kept as heirlooms, or in museums, or that were owned by savage tribes who could procure no ammunition for them, since we permitted none to be manufactured. There was not a gas shell nor a radio bomb, nor any engine to discharge or project one; and there wasn't a big gun of any calibre in the world. I veritably believed that a thousand men equipped with the various engines of destruction that had reached their highest efficiency at the close of the war in 1967 could have conquered the world; but there were not a thousand men so armed—there never could be a thousand men so equipped anywhere upon the face of the Earth. The International Peace Fleet was equipped and manned to prevent just such a calamity.

But it seems that Providence never intended that the world should be without calamities. If man prevented those of possible internal origin there still remained undreamed of external sources over which he had no control. It was one of these which was to prove our undoing. Its seed was sown thirty-three years before I was born, upon that historic day, June 10th, 1967, that Earth received her first message from Mars, since which the two planets have remained in constant friendly communication, carrying on a commerce of reciprocal enlightenment. In some branches of the arts and sciences the Martians, or Barsoomians, as they call themselves, were far in advance of us, while in others we had progressed more rapidly than they. Knowledge was thus freely exchanged to the advantage of both worlds. We learned of their history and customs and they of ours, though they had for ages already known much more of us than we of them. Martian news held always a prominent place in our daily papers from the first.

They helped us most, perhaps, in the fields of medicine and aeronautics, giving us in one, the marvelous healing lotions of Barsoom and in the other, knowledge of the Eighth Ray, which is more generally known on Earth as the Barsoomian Ray, which is now stored in the buoyancy tanks of every air craft and has made obsolete those ancient types of plane that depended upon momentum to keep them afloat.

That we ever were able to communicate intelligibly with them is due to the presence upon Mars of that deathless Virginian, John Carter, whose miraculous transportation to Mars occurred March 4th, 1866, as every school child of the twenty-first century knows. Had not the little band of Martian scientists, who sought so long to communicate with Earth, mistakenly formed themselves into a secret organization for political purposes, messages might have been exchanged between the two planets nearly half a century before they were, and it was not until they finally called upon John Carter that the present inter-planetary code was evolved.

Almost from the first the subject which engrossed us all the most was the possibility of an actual exchange of visits between Earth Men and Barsoomians.

Edgar Rice Burroughs

Each planet hoped to be the first to achieve this, yet neither withheld any information that would aid the other in the consummation of the great fact. It was a generous and friendly rivalry which about the time of my graduation from the Air School seemed, in theory at least, to be almost ripe for successful consummation by one or the other. We had the Eighth Ray, the motors, the oxygenating devices, the insulating processes—everything to insure the safe and certain transit of a specially designed air craft to Mars, were Mars the only other inhabitant of space. But it was not and it was the other planets and the Sun that we feared.

In 2015 Mars had dispatched a ship for Earth with a crew of five men provisioned for ten years. It was hoped that with good luck the trip might be made in something less than five years, as the craft had developed an actual trial speed of one thousand miles per hour. At the time of my graduation the ship was already off its course almost a million miles and generally conceded to be hopelessly lost. Its crew, maintaining constant radio communication with both Earth and Mars, still hoped for success, but the best informed upon both worlds had given them up.

We had had a ship about ready at the time of the sailing of the Martians, but the government at Washington had forbidden the venture when it became apparent that the Barsoomian ship was doomed—a wise decision, since our vessel was no better equipped than theirs. Nearly ten years elapsed before anything further was accomplished in the direction of assuring any greater hope of success for another interplanetary venture into space, and this was directly due to the discovery made by a former classmate of mine, Lieutenant Commander Orthis, one of the most brilliant men I have ever known, and at the same time one of the most unscrupulous, and, to me at least, the most obnoxious.

We had entered the Air School together—he from New York and I from Illinois—and almost from the first day we had seemed to discover a mutual antagonism that, upon his part at least, must have been considerably strengthened by numerous unfortunate occurrences during our four years beneath the same roof. In the first place he was not popular with either the cadets, the instructors, or the officers of the school, while I was most fortunate in this respect. In those various fields of athletics in which he considered himself particularly expert, it was always I, unfortunately, who excelled him and kept him from major honors. In the class room he outshone us all—even the instructors were amazed at the brilliancy of his intellect—and yet as we passed from grade to grade I often topped him in the final examinations. I ranked him always as a cadet officer, and upon graduation I took a higher grade among the new ensigns than he—a rank that had many years before been discontinued, but which had recently been revived.

From then on I saw little of him, his services confining him principally to land service, while mine kept me almost constantly on the air in all parts of the world. Occasionally I heard of him—usually something unsavory; he had married a nice girl and abandoned her—there had been talk of an investigation of his accounts—and the last that there was a rumor that he was affiliated with a secret order that sought to overthrow the government. Some things I might believe of Orthis, but not this.

And during these nine years since graduation, as we had drifted apart in interests, so had the breach between us been widened by constantly increasing difference in rank. He was a Lieutenant Commander and I a Captain, when in 2024 he announced the discovery and isolation of the Eighth Solar Ray, and within two months those of the Moon, Mercury, Venus and Jupiter. The Eighth Barsoomian and the Eighth Earthly Rays had already been isolated, and upon Earth the latter erroneously called by the name of the former.

Orthis' discoveries were hailed upon two planets as the key to actual travel between the Earth and Barsoom, since by means of these several rays the attraction of the Sun and the planets, with the exception of Saturn, Uranus and Neptune, could be definitely overcome and a ship steer a direct and unimpeded course through space to Mars. The effect of the pull of the three farther planets was considered negligible, owing to their great distance from both Mars and Earth.

Orthis wanted to equip a ship and start at once, but again government intervened and forbade what it considered an unnecessary risk. Instead Orthis was ordered to design a small radio operated flier, which would carry no one aboard, and which it was believed could be automatically operated for at least half the distance between the two planets. After his designs were completed, you may imagine his chagrin, and mine as well, when I was detailed to supervise construction, yet I will say that Orthis hid his natural emotions well and gave me perfect cooperation in the work we were compelled to undertake together, and which was as distasteful to me as to him. On my part I made it as easy for him as I could, working with him rather than over him.

It required but a short time to complete the experimental ship and during this time I had an opportunity to get a still better insight into the marvelous intellectual ability of Orthis, though I never saw into his mind or heart.

It was late in 2024 that the ship was launched upon its strange voyage, and almost immediately, upon my recommendation, work was started upon the perfection of the larger ship that had been in course of construction in 2015 at the time that the loss of the Martian ship had discouraged our government in making any further attempt until the then seemingly insurmountable obstacles should have been overcome. Orthis was again my assistant, and with the means at our disposal it was a matter of less than eight months before The Barsoom, as she was christened, was completely overhauled and thoroughly equipped for the interplanetary voyage. The various eighth rays that would assist us in overcoming the pull of the Sun, Mercury, Venus, Earth, Mars and Jupiter were stored in carefully constructed and well protected tanks within the hull, and there was a smaller tank at the bow containing the Eighth Lunar Ray, which would permit us to pass safely within the zone of the moon's influence without danger of being attracted to her barren surface.

Messages from the original Martian ship had been received from time to time and with diminishing strength for nearly five years after it had left Mars. Its commander in his heroic fight against the pull of the sun had managed to fall within the grip of Jupiter and was, when last heard from, far out in the great void between that planet and Mars. During the past four years the fate of the ship could be naught but conjecture—all that we could be certain of was that its unfortunate crew would never again return to Barsoom.

Our own experimental ship had been speeding upon its lonely way now for eight months, and so accurate had Orthis' scientific deductions proven that the most delicate instrument could detect no slightest deviation from its prescribed course. It was then that Orthis began to importune the government to permit him to set out with the new craft that was now completed. The authorities held out, however, until the latter part of 2025 when, the experimental ship having been out a year and still showing no deviation from its course, they felt reasonably assured that the success of the venture was certain and that no useless risk of human life would be involved.

The Barsoom required five men properly to handle it, and as had been the custom through many centuries when an undertaking of more than usual risk was to be attempted, volunteers were called for, with the result that fully half the personnel of the International Peace Fleet begged to be permitted to form the crew of five.

The government finally selected their men from the great number of volunteers, with the result that once more was I the innocent cause of disappointment and chagrin to Orthis, as I was placed in command, with Orthis, two lieutenants and an ensign completing the roster.

The Barsoom was larger than the craft dispatched by the Martians, with the result that we were able to carry supplies for fifteen years. We were equipped with more powerful motors which would permit us to maintain an average speed of over twelve hundred miles an hour, carrying in addition an engine recently developed by Orthis which generated sufficient power from light to propel the craft at half-speed in the event that our other engine should break down. None of us was married, Orthis' abandoned wife having recently died. Our estates were taken under trusteeship by the government. Our farewells were made at an elaborate ball at the White House on December 24, 2025, and on Christmas day we rose from the landing stage at which the Barsoom had been moored, and amid the blare of bands and the shouting of thousands of our fellow countrymen we arose majestically into the blue.

I shall not bore you with dry, technical descriptions of our motors and equipment. Suffice it to say that the former were of three types— those which propelled the ship through the air and those which propelled it through ether, the latter of course represented our most important equipment, and consisted of powerful multiple-exhaust separators which isolated the true Barsoomian Eighth Ray in great quantities, and, by exhausting it rapidly earthward, propelled the vessel toward Mars. These separators were so designed that, with equal facility, they could isolate the Earthly Eighth Ray which would be necessary for our return voyage. The auxiliary engine, which I mentioned previously and which was Orthis' latest invention, could be easily adjusted to isolate the eighth ray of any planet or satellite or of the sun itself, thus insuring us motive power in any part of the universe by the simple expedient of generating and exhausting the eighth ray of the nearest heavenly body. A fourth type of generator drew oxygen from the ether, while another emanated insulating rays which insured us a uniform temperature and external pressure at all times, their action being analogous to that of the atmosphere surrounding the earth. Science had, therefore, permitted us to construct a little world, which moved at will through space—a little world inhabited by five souls.

Had it not been for Orthis' presence I could have looked forward to a reasonably pleasurable voyage, for West and Jay were extremely likeable fellows and sufficiently mature to be companionable, while young Norton, the ensign, though but seventeen years of age, endeared himself to all of us from the very start of the voyage by his pleasant manners, his consideration and his willingness in the performance of his duties. There were three staterooms aboard the Barsoom, one of which I occupied alone, while West and Orthis had the second and Jay and Norton the third. West and Jay were lieutenants and had been classmates at the air school. They would of course have preferred to room together, but could not unless I commanded it or Orthis requested it. Not wishing to give Orthis any grounds for offense I hesitated to make the change, while Orthis, never having thought a considerate thought or done a considerate deed in his life, could not, of course, have been expected to suggest it. We all messed together, West, Jay and Norton taking turns at preparing the meals. Only in the actual operation of the ship were the lines of rank drawn strictly. Otherwise we associated as equals, nor would any other arrangement have been endurable upon such an undertaking, which required that we five be practically imprisoned together upon a small ship for a period of not less than five years. We had books and writing materials and games, and we were, of course, in constant radio communication with both Earth and Mars, receiving continuously the latest news from both planets. We listened to opera and oratory and heard the music of two worlds, so that we were not lacking for entertainment. There was always a certain constraint in Orthis' manner toward me, yet I must give him credit for behaving outwardly admirably. Unlike the others we never exchanged pleasantries with one another, nor could I, knowing as I did that Orthis hated me, and feeling for him personally the contempt that I felt because of his character. Intellectually he commanded my highest admiration, and upon intellectual grounds we met without constraint or reserve, and many were the profitable discussions we had during the first days of what was to prove a very brief voyage.

It was about the second day that I noticed with some surprise that Orthis was exhibiting a friendly interest in Norton. It had never been Orthis' way to make friends, but I saw that he and Norton were much together and that each seemed to derive a great deal of pleasure from the society of the other. Orthis was a good talker. He knew his profession thoroughly, and was an inventor and scientist of high distinction. Norton, though but a boy, was himself the possessor of a fine mind. He had been honor-man in his graduating class, heading the list of ensigns for that year, and I could not help but notice that he was drinking in every word along scientific lines that Orthis vouchsafed.

We had been out about six days when Orthis came to me and suggested, that inasmuch as West and Jay had been classmates and chums that they be permitted to room together and that he had spoken to Norton who had said that he would be agreeable to the change and would occupy West's bunk in Orthis' stateroom. I was very glad of this for it now meant that my subordinates would be paired off in the most agreeable manner, and as long as they were contented, I knew that the voyage from that standpoint at least would be more successful. I was, of course, a trifle sorry to see a fine boy like Norton brought under the influence of Orthis, yet I felt that what little danger might result would be offset by the influence of West and Jay and myself or counter-balanced by the liberal education which five years' constant companionship with Orthis would be to any man with whom Orthis would discuss freely the subjects of which he was master.

We were beginning to feel the influence of the Moon rather strongly. At the rate we were traveling we would pass closest to it upon the twelfth day, or about the 6th of January, 2026.

Our course would bring us within about twenty thousand miles of the Moon, and as we neared it I believe that the sight of it was the most impressive thing that human eye had ever gazed upon before. To the naked eye it loomed large and magnificent in the heavens, appearing over ten times the size that it does to terrestrial observers, while our powerful glasses brought its weird surface to such startling proximity that one felt that he might reach out and touch the torn rocks of its tortured mountains.

This nearer view enabled us to discover the truth or falsity of the theory that has been long held by some scientists that there is a form of vegetation upon the surface of the Moon. Our eyes were first attracted by what appeared to be movement upon the surface of some of the valleys and in the deeper ravines of the mountains. Norton exclaimed that there were creatures there, moving about, but closer observation revealed the fact of the existence of a weird fungus-like vegetation which grew so rapidly that we could clearly discern the phenomena. From the several days' observation which we had at close range we came to the conclusion that the entire life span of this vegetation is encompassed in a single sidereal month. From the spore it developed in the short period of a trifle over twenty-seven days into a mighty plant that is sometimes hundreds of feet in height. The branches are angular and grotesque, the leaves broad and thick, and in the plants which we discerned the seven primary colors were distinctly represented. As each portion of the Moon passed slowly into shadow the vegetation first drooped, then wilted, then crumbled to the ground, apparently disintegrating almost immediately into a fine, dust-like powder—at least in so far as our glasses revealed, it quite disappeared entirely. The movement which we discerned was purely that of rapid growth, as there is no wind upon the surface of the Moon. Both Jay and Orthis were positive that they discerned some form of animal life, either insect or reptilian. These I did not myself see, though I did perceive many of the broad, flat leaves which seemed to have been partially eaten, which certainly strengthened the theory that there is other than vegetable life upon our satellite.

I presume that one of the greatest thrills that we experienced in this adventure, that was to prove a veritable Pandora's box of thrills, was when we commenced to creep past the edge of the Moon and our eyes beheld for the first time that which no other human eyes had ever rested upon— portions of that two-fifths of the Moon's surface which is invisible from the Earth.

We had looked with awe upon Mare Crisium and Lacus Somniorum, Sinius Roris, Oceanus Procellarum and the four great mountain ranges. We had viewed at close range the volcanoes of Opollonius, Secchi, Borda, Tycho and their mates, but all these paled into insignificance as there unrolled before us the panorama of the vast unknown.

I cannot say that it differed materially from that portion of the Moon that is visible to us—it was merely the glamour of mystery which had surrounded it since the beginning of time that lent to it its thrill for us. Here we observed other great mountain ranges and wide undulating plains, towering volcanoes and mighty craters and the same vegetation with which we had now become familiar.

We were two days past the Moon when our first trouble developed. Among our stores were one hundred and twenty quarts of spirits per man, enough to allow us each a liberal two ounces per day for a period of five years. Each night, before dinner, we had drunk to the President in a cocktail which contained a single ounce of spirits, the idea being to conserve our supply in the event of our journey being unduly protracted as well as to have enough in the event that it became desirable fittingly to celebrate any particular occasion.

Toward the third meal hour of the thirteenth day of the voyage Orthis entered the messroom noticeably under the influence of liquor.

History narrates that under the regime of prohibition drunkenness was common and that it grew to such proportions as to become a national menace, but with the repeal of the Prohibition Act, nearly a hundred years ago, the habit of drinking to excess abated, so that it became a matter of disgrace for any man to show his liquor, and in the service it was considered as reprehensible as cowardice in action. There was therefore but one thing for me to do. I ordered Orthis to his quarters.

The Moon Maid

He was drunker than I had thought him, and he turned upon me like a tiger.

"You damned cur," he cried. "All my life you have stolen everything from me; the fruits of all my efforts you have garnered by chicanery and trickery, and even now, were we to reach Mars, it is you who would be lauded as the hero—not I whose labor and intellect have made possible this achievement. But by God we will not reach Mars. Not again shall you profit by my efforts. You have gone too far this time, and now you dare to order me about like a dog and an inferior—I, whose brains have made you what you are."

I held my temper, for I saw that the man was unaccountable for his words. "Go to your quarters, Orthis," I repeated my command. "I will talk with you again in the morning."

West and Jay and Norton were present. They seemed momentarily paralyzed by the man's condition and gross insubordination. Norton, however, was the first to recover. Jumping quickly to Orthis' side he laid his hand upon his arm. "Come, sir," he said, and to my surprise Orthis accompanied him quietly to their stateroom.

During the voyage we had continued the fallacy of night and day, gauging them merely by our chronometers, since we moved always through utter darkness, surrounded only by a tiny nebula of light, produced by the sun's rays impinging upon the radiation from our insulating generator. Before breakfast, therefore, on the following morning I sent for Orthis to come to my stateroom. He entered with a truculent swagger, and his first words indicated that if he had not continued drinking, he had at least been moved to no regrets for his unwarranted attack of the previous evening.

"Well," he said, "what in hell are you going to do about it?"

"I cannot understand your attitude, Orthis," I told him. "I have never intentionally injured you. When orders from government threw us together I was as much chagrined as you. Association with you is as distasteful to me as it is to you. I merely did as you did—obeyed orders. I have no desire to rob you of anything, but that is not the question now. You have been guilty of gross insubordination and of drunkenness. I can prevent a repetition of the latter by confiscating your liquor and keeping it from you during the balance of the voyage, and an apology from you will atone for the former. I shall give you twenty-four hours to reach a decision. If you do not see fit to avail yourself of my clemency, Orthis, you will travel to Mars and back again in irons. Your decision now and your behavior during the balance of the voyage will decide your fate upon our return to Earth. And I tell you, Orthis, that if I possibly can do so I shall use the authority which is mine upon this expedition and expunge from the log the record of your transgressions last night and this morning. Now go to your quarters; your meals will be served there for twenty-four hours and at the end of that time I shall receive your decision. Meanwhile your liquor will be taken from you."

He gave me an ugly look, turned upon his heel and left my stateroom.

Norton was on watch that night. We were two days past the Moon. West, Jay and I were asleep in our staterooms, when suddenly Norton entered mine and shook me violently by the shoulder.

"My God, Captain," he cried, "come quick. Commander Orthis is destroying the engines."

I leaped to my feet and followed Norton amidships to the engine-room, calling to West and Jay as I passed their state-room. Through the bull's-eye in the engine-room door, which he had locked, we could see Orthis working over the auxiliary generator which was to have proven our salvation in an emergency, since by means of it we could overcome the pull of any planet into the sphere of whose influence we might be carried. I breathed a sigh of relief as my eyes noted that the main battery of engines was functioning properly, since, as a matter of fact, we had not expected to have to rely at all upon the auxiliary generator, having stored sufficient quantities of the Eighth Ray of the various heavenly bodies by which we might be influenced, to carry us safely throughout the entire extent of the long voyage. West and Jay had joined us by this time, and I now called to Orthis, commanding him to open the door. He did something more to the generator and then arose, crossed the engine-room directly to the door, unbolted it and threw the door open. His hair was dishevelled, his face drawn, his eyes shining with a peculiar light, but withal his expression denoted a drunken elation that I did not at the moment understand.

"What have you been doing here, Orthis?" I demanded. "You are under arrest, and supposed to be in your quarters."

"You'll see what I've been doing," he replied truculently, "and it's done —it's done—it can't ever be undone. I've seen to that."

I grabbed him roughly by the shoulder. "What do you mean? Tell me what you have done, or by God I will kill you with my own hands," for I knew, not only from his words but from his expression, that he had accomplished something which he considered very terrible.

The man was a coward and he quailed under my grasp. "You wouldn't dare to kill me," he cried, "and it don't make any difference, for we'll all be dead in a few hours. Go and look at your damned compass."

The Secret of the Moon

NORTON, whose watch it was, had already hurried toward the pilot room where were located the controls and the various instruments. This room, which was just forward of the engine-room, was in effect a circular conning-tower which projected about twelve inches above the upper hull. The entire circumference of this twelve inch superstructure was set with small ports of thick crystal glass.

As I turned to follow Norton I spoke to West. "Mr. West," I said, "you and Mr. Jay will place Lieutenant Commander Orthis in irons immediately. If he resists, kill him."

As I hurried after Norton I heard a volley of oaths from Orthis and a burst of almost maniacal laughter. When I reached the pilot house I found Norton working very quietly with the controls. There was nothing hysterical in his movements, but his face was absolutely ashen.

"What is wrong, Mr. Norton?" I asked. But as I looked at the compass simultaneously I read my answer there before he spoke. We were moving at right angles to our proper course.

"We are falling toward the Moon, sir," he said, "and she does not respond to her control."

"Shut down the engines," I ordered, "they are only accelerating our fall,"

"Aye, aye, sir," he replied.

"The Lunar Eighth Ray tank is of sufficient capacity to keep us off the Moon," I said. "If it has not been tampered with, we should be in no danger of falling to the Moon's surface."

"If it has not been tampered with, sir; yes, sir, that is what I have been thinking."

"But the gauge here shows it full to capacity," I reminded him.

"I know, sir," he replied, "but if it were full to capacity, we should not be falling so rapidly."

Immediately I fell to examining the gauge, almost at once discovering that it had been tampered with and the needle set permanently to indicate a maximum supply. I turned to my companion.

"Mr. Norton," I said, "please go forward and investigate the Lunar Eighth Ray tank, and report back to me immediately."

The young man saluted and departed. As he approached the tank it was necessary for him to crawl through a very restricted place beneath the deck.

In about five minutes Norton returned. He was not so pale as he had been, but he looked very haggard.

"Well?" I inquired as he halted before me.

"The exterior intake valve has been opened, sir," he said, "the rays were escaping into space. I have closed it, sir."

The valve to which he referred was used only when the ship was in dry dock, for the purpose of refilling the buoyancy tank, and, because it was so seldom used and as a further precaution against accident, the valve was placed in an inaccessible part of the hull where there was absolutely no likelihood of its being accidentally opened.

Norton glanced at the instrument. "We are not falling quite so rapidly now," he said.

"Yes," I replied, "I had noted that, and I have also been able to adjust the Lunar Eighth Ray gauge—it shows that we have about half the original pressure."

"Not enough to keep us from going aground," he commented.

"No, not here, where there is no atmosphere. If the Moon had an atmosphere we could at least keep off the surface if we wished to. As it is, however, I imagine that we will be able to make a safe landing, though, of course that will do us little good. You understand, I suppose, Mr. Norton, that this is practically the end."

He nodded. "It will be a sad blow to the inhabitants of two worlds," he remarked, his entire forgetfulness of self indicating the true nobility of his character.

"It is a sad report to broadcast," I remarked, "but it must be done, and at once. You will, please, send the following message to the Secretary of Peace:

"U.S.S. the Barsoom, January 6, 2026, about twenty thousand miles off the Moon. Lieutenant Commander Orthis, while under the influence of liquor, has destroyed auxiliary engine and opened exterior intake valve Lunar Eighth Ray buoyancy tank. Ship sinking rapidly. Will keep you—"

Norton who had seated himself at the radio desk leaped suddenly to his feet and turned toward me. "My God, sir," he cried, "he has destroyed the radio outfit also. We can neither send nor receive."

A careful examination revealed the fact that Orthis had so cleverly and completely destroyed the instruments that there was no hope of repairing them. I turned to Norton.

"We are not only dead, Norton, but we are buried, as well."

I smiled as I spoke and he answered me with a smile that betokened his utter fearlessness of death.

"I have but one regret, sir," he said, "and that is that the world will never know that our failure was not due to any weakness of our machinery, ship or equipment."

"That is, indeed, too bad," I replied, "for it will retard transportation between the two worlds possibly a hundred years—maybe forever."

I called to West and Jay who by this time had placed Orthis in irons and confined him to his stateroom. When they came I told them what had happened, and they took it as coolly as did Norton. Nor was I surprised, for these were fine types selected from the best of that splendid organization which officered the International Peace Fleet.

Together we immediately made a careful inspection of the ship, which revealed no further damage than that which we had already discovered, but which was sufficient as we well knew, to preclude any possibility of our escaping from the pull of the Moon.

"You gentlemen realize our position as well as I," I told them. "Could we repair the auxiliary generator we might isolate the Lunar Eighth Ray, refill our tank, and resume our voyage. But the diabolical cleverness with which Lieutenant Commander Orthis has wrecked the machine renders this impossible. We might fight away from the surface of the Moon for a considerable period, but in the end it would avail us nothing. It is my plan, therefore, to make a landing. In so far as the actual lunar conditions are concerned, we are confronted only by a mass of theories, many of which are conflicting. It will, therefore, be at least a matter of consuming interest to us to make a landing upon this dead world where we may observe it closely, but there is also the possibility, remote, I grant you, that we may discover conditions there which may in some manner alleviate our position. At least we can be no worse off. To live for fifteen years cooped in the hull of this dead ship is unthinkable. I may speak only for myself, but to me it would be highly preferable to die immediately than to live on thus, knowing that there was no hope of rescue. Had Orthis not destroyed the radio outfit we could have communicated with Earth and another ship been outfitted and sent to our rescue inside a year. But now we cannot tell them, and they will never know our fate. The emergency that has arisen has, however, so altered conditions that I do not feel warranted in taking this step without consulting you gentlemen. It is a matter now largely of the duration of our lives. I cannot proceed upon the mission upon which I have been dispatched, nor can I return to Earth. I wish, therefore, that you would express yourselves freely concerning the plan which I have outlined."

West, who was the senior among them, was naturally the one to reply first. He told me that he was content to go wherever I led, and Jay and Norton in turn signified a similar willingness to abide by whatever decision I might reach. They also assured me that they were as keen to explore the surface of the Moon at close range as I, and that they could think of no better way of spending the remainder of their lives than in the acquisition of new experiences and the observation of new scenes.

"Very well, Mr. Norton," I said, "you will set your course directly toward the Moon."

Aided by lunar gravity our descent was rapid.

As we plunged through space at a terrific speed, the satellite seemed to be leaping madly toward us, and at the end of fifteen hours I gave orders to slack off and brought the ship almost to a stop about nine thousand feet above the summit of the higher lunar peaks. Never before had I gazed upon a more awe-inspiring scene than that presented by those terrific peaks towering five miles above the broad valleys at their feet. Sheer cliffs of three and four thousand feet were nothing uncommon, and all was rendered weirdly beautiful by the variegated colors of the rocks and the strange prismatic hues of the rapidly-growing vegetation upon the valley floors. From our lofty elevation above the peaks we could see many craters of various dimensions, some of which were huge chasms, three and four miles in diameter. As we descended slowly we drifted directly over one of these abysses, into the impenetrable depths of which we sought to strain our eyesight. Some of us believed that we detected a faint luminosity far below, but of that we could not be certain. Jay thought it might be the reflected light from the molten interior. I was confident that had this been the case there would have been a considerable rise of temperature as we passed low across the mouth of the crater.

At this altitude we made an interesting discovery. There is an atmosphere surrounding the Moon. It is extremely tenuous, but yet it was recorded by our barometer at an altitude of about fifteen hundred feet above the highest peak we crossed. Doubtless in the valleys and deep ravines, where the vegetation thrived, it is denser, but that I do not know, since we never landed upon the surface of the

Moon. As the ship drifted we presently noted that it was taking a circular course paralleling the rim of the huge volcanic crater above which we were descending. I immediately gave orders to alter our course since, as we were descending constantly, we should presently be below the rim of the crater and, being unable to rise, be hopelessly lost in its huge maw.

It was my plan to drift slowly over one of the larger valleys as we descended, and make a landing amidst the vegetation which we perceived growing in riotous profusion and movement beneath us. But when West, whose watch it now was, attempted to alter the course of the ship, he found that it did not respond. Instead it continued to move slowly in a great circle around the inside rim of the crater. At the moment of this discovery we were not much more than five hundred feet above the summit of the volcano, and we were constantly, though slowly, dropping. West looked up at us, smiled, and shook his head.

"It is no use, sir," he said, addressing me. "It is about all over, sir, and there won't even be any shouting. We seem to be caught in what one might call a lunar whirlpool, for you will have noticed, sir, that our circles are constantly growing smaller."

"Our speed does not seem to be increasing," I remarked, "as would follow were we approaching the vortex of a true whirlpool."

"I think I can explain it, sir," said Norton. "It is merely due to the action of the Lunar Eighth Ray which still remains in the forward buoyancy tank. Its natural tendency is to push itself away from the Moon, which, as far as we are concerned, is represented by the rim of this enormous crater. As each portion of the surface repels us in its turn we are pushed gently along in a lessening circle, because, as we drop nearer the summit of the peak the greater the reaction of the Eighth Lunar Ray. If I am not mistaken in my theory our circle will cease to narrow after we have dropped beneath the rim of the crater."

"I guess you are right, Norton," I said. "At least it is a far more tenable theory than that we are being sucked into the vortex of an enormous whirlpool. There is scarcely enough atmosphere for that, it seems to me."

As we dropped slowly below the rim of the crater the tenability of Norton's theory became more and more apparent, for presently, though our speed increased slightly, the diameter of our circular course remained constant, and, at a little greater depth, our speed as well. We were descending now at the rate of a little over ten miles an hour, the barometer recording a constantly increasing atmospheric pressure, though nothing approximating that necessary to the support of life upon Earth. The temperature rose slightly, but not alarmingly. From a range of twenty-five or thirty below zero, immediately after we had entered the shadow of the crater's interior, it rose gradually to zero at a point some one hundred and twenty-five miles below the summit of the giant extinct volcano that had engulfed us.

During the next ten miles our speed diminished rapidly, until we suddenly realized that we were no longer falling, but that our motion had been reversed and we were rising. Up we went for approximately eight miles, when suddenly we began to fall again. Again we fell, but this time for only six miles, when our motion was reversed and we rose again a distance of about four miles. This see-sawing was continued until we finally came to rest at about what we estimated was a distance of some one hundred and thirty miles below the summit of the crater. It was quite dark, and we had only our instruments to tell us of what was happening to the ship, the interior of which was, of course, brilliantly illuminated and comfortably warm.

Now below us, and now above us, for the ship had rolled completely over each time we had passed the point at which we came finally to rest, we had noted the luminosity that Norton had first observed from above the mouth of the crater. Each of us had been doing considerable thinking, and at last young Norton could contain himself no longer.

"I beg your pardon, sir," he said deferentially, "but won't you tell us what you think of it; what your theory is as to where we are and why we hang here in mid-air, and why the ship rolled over every time we passed this point?"

"I can only account for it," I replied, "upon a single and rather preposterous hypothesis, which is that the Moon is a hollow sphere, with a solid crust some two hundred and fifty miles in thickness. Gravity is preventing us from rising above the point where we now are, while centrifugal force keeps us from falling."

The others nodded. They too had been forced to accept the same apparently ridiculous theory, since there was none other that could explain our predicament. Norton had walked across the room to read the barometer which he had rather neglected while the ship had been performing her eccentric antics far below the surface of the Moon. I saw his brows knit as he glanced at it, and then I saw him studying it carefully, as though to assure himself that he had made no mistake in the reading. Then he turned toward us.

"There must be something wrong with this instrument, sir," he said. "It is registering pressure equivalent to that at the Earth's surface."

The Moon Maid

I walked over and looked at the instrument. It certainly was registering the pressure that Norton had read, nor did there seem to be anything wrong with the instrument.

"There is a way to find out," I said. "We can shut down the insulating generator and open an air-cock momentarily. It won't take five seconds to determine whether the barometer is correct or not." It was, of course, in some respects a risky proceeding, but with West at the generator, Jay at the air-cock and Norton at the pump I knew that we would be reasonably safe, even if there proved to be no atmosphere without. The only danger lay in the chance that we were hanging in a poisonous gas of the same density as the earthly atmosphere, but as there was no particular incentive to live in the situation in which we were, we each felt that no matter what chance we might take it would make little difference in the eventual outcome of our expedition.

I tell you that it was a very tense moment as the three men took their posts to await my word of command. If we had indeed discovered a true atmosphere beneath the surface of the Moon, what more might we not discover? If it were an atmosphere, we could propel the ship in it, and we could, if nothing more, go out on deck to breathe fresh air. It was arranged that at my word of command West was to shut off the generator. Jay to open the air-cock, and Norton to start the pump. If fresh air failed to enter through the tube Jay was to give the signal, whereupon Norton would reverse the pump, West start the generator, and immediately Jay would close the air-cock again.

As Jay was the only man who was to take a greater chance than the others, I walked over and stood beside him, placing my nostrils as close to the air-cock as his. Then I gave the word of command. Everything worked perfectly and an instant later a rush of fresh, cold air was pouring into the hull of the Barsoom. West and Norton had been watching the effects upon our faces closely, so that they knew almost as soon as we did that the result of our test had been satisfactory. We were all smiles, though just why we were so happy I am sure none of us could have told. Possibly it was just because we had found a condition that was identical with an earthly condition, and though we might never see our world again we could at least breathe air similar to hers. I had them start the motors again then, and presently we were moving in a great spiral upward toward the interior of the Moon. Our progress was very slow, but as we rose the temperature rose slowly, too, while the barometer showed a very-slightly-decreasing atmospheric pressure. The luminosity, now above us, increased as we ascended, until finally the sides of the great well through which we were passing became slightly illuminated.

All this time Orthis had remained in irons in his stateroom. I had given instructions that he was to be furnished food and water, but no one was to speak to him, and I had taken Norton into my stateroom with me. Knowing Orthis to be a drunkard, a traitor and a potential murderer I had no sympathy whatsoever for him. I had determined to court-martial him and did not intend to spend the few remaining hours or years of my life cooped up in a small ship with him, and I knew that the verdict of any court, whether composed of the remaining crew of the Barsoom, or appointed by the Judge Advocate General of the Navy, could result in but one thing, and that was death for Orthis. I had left the matter, however, until we were not pressed with other matters of greater importance, and so he still lived, though he shared neither in our fears, our hopes, nor our joys.

About twenty-six hours after we entered the mouth of the crater at the surface of the Moon we suddenly emerged from its opposite end to look upon a scene that was as marvelous and weird, by comparison with the landscape upon the surface of the Moon, as the latter was in comparison with that of our own Earth. A soft, diffused light revealed to us in turn mountains, valleys and sea, the details of which were more slowly encompassed by our minds. The mountains were as rugged as those upon the surface of the satellite, and appeared equally as lofty. They were, however, clothed with verdure almost to their summits, at least a few that were within our range of vision. And there were forests, too—strange forests, of strange trees, so unearthly in appearance as to suggest the weird phantasmagoria of a dream.

We did not rise much above five hundred feet from the opening of the well through which we had come from outer space when I descried an excellent landing place and determined to descend. This was readily accomplished, and we made a safe landing close to a large forest and near the bank of a small stream. Then we opened the forward hatch and stepped out upon the deck of the Barsoom, the first Earth Men to breathe the air of Luna. It was, according to Earth time, eleven A.M., January 8, 2026.

I think that the first thing which engaged our interest and attention was the strange, and then, to us, unaccountable luminosity which pervaded the interior of the Moon. Above us were banks of fleecy clouds, the undersurfaces of which appeared to be lighted from beneath, while, through breaks in the cloud banks we could discern a luminous firmament beyond, though nowhere was there any

The Moon Maid

suggestion of a central incandescent orb radiating light and heat as does our sun. The clouds themselves cast no shadows upon the ground, nor, in fact, were there any well-defined shadows even directly beneath the hull of the ship or surrounding the forest trees which grew close at hand. The shadows were vague and nebulous, blending off into nothingnesses at their edges. We ourselves cast no more shadows upon the deck of the Barsoom than would have been true upon a cloudy day on Earth. Yet the general illumination surrounding us approximated that of a very slightly hazy Earth day. This peculiar lunar light interested us profoundly, but it was some time before we discovered the true explanation of its origin. It was of two kinds, emanating from widely different sources, the chief of which was due to the considerable radium content of the internal lunar soil, and principally of the rock forming the loftier mountain ranges, the radium being so combined as to diffuse a gentle perpetual light which pervaded the entire interior of the Moon. The secondary source was sunlight, which penetrated to the interior of the Moon through the hundreds of thousands of huge craters penetrating the lunar crust. It was this sunlight which carried heat to the inner world, maintaining a constant temperature of about eighty degrees Fahrenheit.

Centrifugal force, in combination with the gravity of the Moon's crust, confined the internal lunar atmosphere to a blanket which we estimated at about fifty miles in thickness over the inner surface of this buried world. This atmosphere rarefies rapidly as one ascends the higher peaks, with the result that these are constantly covered with perpetual snow and ice, sending great glaciers down mighty gorges toward the central seas. It is this condition which has probably prevented the atmosphere, confined as it is within an almost solid sphere, from becoming superheated, through the unthinkable ages that this condition must have existed. The Earth seasons are reflected but slightly in the Moon, there being but a few degrees difference between summer and winter. There are, however, periodic wind-storms, which recur with greater or less regularity once each sidereal month, due, I imagine, to the unequal distribution of crater openings through the crust of the Moon, a fact which must produce an unequal absorption of heat at various times and in certain localities. The natural circulation of the lunar atmosphere, affected as it is by the constantly-changing volume and direction of the sun's rays, as well as the great range of temperature between the valleys and the ice-clad mountain peaks, produces frequent storms of greater or less violence. High winds are accompanied by violent rains upon the lower levels and blinding snowstorms among the barren heights above the vegetation line. Rains which fall from low-hanging clouds are warm and pleasant; those which come from high clouds are cold and disagreeable, yet however violent or protracted the storm, the illumination remains practically constant— there are never any dark, lowering days within the Moon, nor is there any night.

Animals or Men?

OF course we did not reach all these conclusions in a few moments, but I have given them here merely as the outcome of our deductions following a considerable experience within the Moon. Several miles from the ship rose foothills which climbed picturesquely toward the cloudy heights of the loftier mountains behind them, and as we looked in the direction of these latter, and then out across the forest, there was appreciable to us a strangeness that at first we could not explain, but which we later discovered was due to the fact that there was no horizon, the distance that one could see being dependent solely upon one's power of vision. The general effect was of being in the bottom of a tremendous bowl, with sides so high that one might not see the top.

The ground about us was covered with rank vegetation of pale hues—lavenders, violets, pinks and yellows predominating. Pink grasses which became distinctly flesh-color at maturity grew in abundance, and the stalks of most of the flowering plants were of this same peculiar hue. The flowers themselves were often of highly complex form, of pale and delicate shades, of great size and rare beauty. There were low shrubs that bore a berry-like fruit, and many of the trees of the forest carried fruit of considerable size and of a variety of forms and colors. Norton and Jay were debating the possible edibility of some of these, but I gave orders that no one was to taste them until we had had an opportunity to learn by analysis or otherwise those varieties that were non-poisonous.

There was aboard the Barsoom a small laboratory equipped especially for the purpose of analyzing the vegetable and mineral products of Mars according to earthly standards, as well as other means of conducting research work upon our sister planet. As we had sufficient food aboard for a period of fifteen years, there was no immediate necessity for eating any of the lunar fruit, but I was anxious to ascertain the chemical properties of the water since the manufacture of this necessity was slow, laborious and expensive. I therefore instructed West to take a sample from the stream and subject it to laboratory tests, and the others I ordered below for sleep.

They were rather more keen to set out upon a tour of exploration, nor could I blame them, but as none of us had slept for rather better than forty-eight hours I considered it of importance that we recuperate our vital forces against whatever contingency might confront us in this unknown world. Here were air, water and vegetation—the three prime requisites for the support of animal life—and so I judged it only reasonable to assume that animal life existed within the Moon. If it did exist, it might be in some highly predatory form, against which it would tax our resources to the utmost to defend ourselves. I insisted, therefore, upon each of us obtaining his full quota of sleep before venturing from the safety of the Barsoom.

We already had seen evidences of life of a low order, both reptile and insect, or perhaps it would be better to describe the latter as flying reptiles, as they later proved to be—toad-like creatures with the wings of bats, that flitted among the fleshy boughs of the forest, emitting plaintive cries. Upon the ground near the ship we had seen but a single creature, though the moving grasses had assured us that there were others there aplenty. The thing that we had seen had been plainly visible to us all and may be best described as a five-foot snake with four frog-like legs, and a flat head with a single eye in the center of the forehead. Its legs were very short, and as it moved along the ground it both wriggled like a true snake and scrambled with its four short legs. We watched it to the edge of the river and saw it dive in and disappear beneath the surface.

"Silly looking beggar," remarked Jay, "and devilish unearthly."

"I don't know about that," I returned. "He possessed nothing visible to us that we are not familiar with on Earth. Possibly he was assembled after a slightly different plan from any Earth creature; but aside from that he is familiar to us, even to his amphibious habits. And these flying toads, too; what of them? I see nothing particularly remarkable about them. We have just as strange forms on Earth, though nothing precisely like these. Mars, too, has forms of animal and vegetable life peculiar to herself, yet nothing the existence of which would be impossible upon Earth, and she has, as well, human forms almost identical with our own. You see what I am trying to suggest?"

"Yes, sir," replied Jay; "that there may be human life similar to our own within the Moon."

"I see no reason to be surprised should we discover human beings here," I said;

"nor would I be surprised to find a reasoning creature of some widely divergent form. I would be surprised, however, were we to find no form analogous to the human race of Earth."

"That is, a dominant race with well developed reasoning faculties?" asked Norton.

"Yes, and it is because of this possibility that we must have sleep and keep ourselves fit, since we may not know the disposition of these creatures, provided they exist, nor the reception that they will accord us. And so, Mr. Norton, if you will get a receptacle and fetch some water from the stream we will leave Mr. West on watch to make his analysis and the rest of us will turn in."

Norton went below and returned with a glass jar in which to carry the water and the balance of us lined the rail with our service revolvers ready in the event of an emergency as he went over the side. None of us had walked more than a few steps since coming on deck after our landing. I had noticed a slightly peculiar sensation of buoyancy, but in view of the numerous other distractions had given it no consideration. As Norton reached the bottom of the ladder and set foot on lunar soil I called to him to make haste. Just in front of him was a low bush and beyond it lay the river, about thirty feet distant. In response to my command he gave a slight leap to clear the bush and, to our amazement as well as to his own consternation, rose fully eighteen feet into the air, cleared a space of fully thirty-five feet and lit in the river.

"Come!" I said to the others, wishing them to follow me to Norton's aid, and sprang for the rail; but I was too impetuous. I never touched the rail, but cleared it by many feet, sailed over the intervening strip of land, and disappeared beneath the icy waters of the lunar river. How deep it was I do not know; but at least it was over my head. I found myself in a sluggish, yet powerful current, the water seeming to move much as a heavy oil moves to the gravity of Earth. As I came to the surface I saw Norton swimming strongly for the bank and a second later Jay emerged not far from me. I glanced quickly around for West, whom I immediately perceived was still on the deck of the Barsoom, where, of course, it was his duty to remain, since it was his watch.

The moment that I realized that my companions were all safe I could not repress a smile, and then Norton and Jay commenced to laugh, and we were still laughing when we pulled ourselves from the stream a short distance below the ship.

"Get your sample, Norton?" I asked.

"I still have the container, sir," he replied, and indeed he had clung to it throughout his surprising adventure, as Jay and I, fortunately, had clung to our revolvers. Norton removed the cap from the bottle and dipped the latter into the stream. Then he looked up at me and smiled.

"I think we have beaten Mr. West to it, sir," he said. "It seems like very good water, sir, and when I struck it I was so surprised that I must have swallowed at least a quart."

"I tested a bit of it myself," I replied. "As far as we three are concerned, Mr. West's analysis will not interest us if he discovers that lunar water contains poisonous matter, but for his own protection we will let him proceed with his investigation."

"It is strange, sir," remarked Jay, "that none of us thought of the natural effects of the lesser gravity of the Moon. We have discussed the matter upon many occasions, as you will recall, yet when we faced the actual condition we gave it no consideration whatsoever."

"I am glad," remarked Norton, "that I did not attempt to jump the river—I should have been going yet. Probably landed on the top of some mountain."

As we approached the ship I saw West awaiting us with a most serious and dignified mien; but when he saw that we were all laughing he joined us, telling us after we reached the deck, that he had never witnessed a more surprising or ludicrous sight in his life.

We went below then and after closing and securing the hatch, three of us repaired to our bunks, while West with the sample of lunar water went to the laboratory. I was very tired and slept soundly for some ten hours, for it was the middle of Norton's watch before I awoke.

The only important entry upon the log since I had turned in was West's report of the results of his analysis of the water, which showed that it was not only perfectly safe for drinking purposes but unusually pure, with an extremely low saline content.

I had been up about a half an hour when West came to me, saying that Orthis requested permission to speak to me. Twenty-four hours before, I had been fairly well determined to bring Orthis to trial and execute him immediately, but that had been when I had felt that we were all hopelessly doomed to death on his account. Now, however, with a habitable world beneath our feet, surrounded by conditions almost identical with those which existed upon Earth, our future looked less dark, and because of this I found myself in a quandary as to what course of action to pursue in the matter of Orthis' punishment. That he deserved death there was no question, but when men have faced death so closely and escaped, temporarily at least, I believe that they must look upon life as a most sacred thing and be less inclined to deny life to others. Be that as it may, the fact remains that having sent for Orthis in compliance with his request I received him in a mood of less stern and uncompromising justice than would have been the case twenty-four hours previous. When he had been brought to my stateroom and stood before me, I asked him what he wished to say to me. He was entirely sober now and bore himself with a certain dignity that was not untinged with humility.

"I do not know what has occurred since I was put in irons, as you have instructed the others not to speak to me or answer my questions. I know, of course, however, that the ship is at rest and that pure air is circulating through it, and I have heard the hatch raised and footsteps upon the upper deck. From the time that has elapsed since I was placed under arrest I know that the only planet upon which we have had time to make a landing is the Moon, and so I may guess that we are upon the surface of the Moon. I have had ample time to reflect upon my actions. That I was intoxicated is, of course, no valid excuse, and yet it is the only excuse that I have to offer. I beg, sir, that you will accept the assurance of my sincere regret of the unforgivable things that I have done, and that you will permit me to live and atone for my wrongdoings, for if we are indeed upon the surface of the Moon it may be that we can ill spare a single member of our small party. I throw myself, sir, entirely upon your mercy, but beg that you will give me another chance."

Realizing my natural antipathy for the man and wishing most sincerely not to be influenced against him because of it, I let his plea influence me against my better judgement with the result that I promised him that I would give the matter careful consideration, discuss it with the others, and be influenced largely by their decision. I had him returned to his stateroom then and sent for the other members of the party. With what fidelity my memory permitted I repeated to them in Orthis' own words his request for mercy.

"And now, gentlemen," I said, "I would like to have your opinions in the matter. It is of as much moment to you as to me, and under the peculiar circumstances in which we are placed, I prefer in so far as possible to defer wherever I can to the judgment of the majority. Whatever my final action, the responsibility will be mine. I do not seek to divide that, and it may be that I shall act contrary to the wishes of the majority in some matters, but in this one I really wish to abide by your desires because of the personal antagonism that has existed between Lieutenant Commander Orthis and myself since boyhood."

The Moon Maid

I knew that none of these men liked Orthis, yet I knew, too, that they would approach the matter in a spirit of justice tempered by mercy, and so I was not at all surprised when one after another they assured me that they would be glad if I would give the man another opportunity.

Again I sent for Orthis, and after explaining to him that inasmuch as he had given me his word to commit no disloyal act in the future I should place him on parole, his eventual fate depending entirely upon his own conduct; then had his irons removed and told him that be was to return to duty. He seemed most grateful and assured us that we would never have cause to regret our decision. Would to God that instead of freeing him I had drawn my revolver and shot him through the heart!

We were all pretty well rested up by this time, and I undertook to do a little exploring in the vicinity of the ship, going out for a few hours each day with a single companion, leaving the other three upon the ship. I never went far afield at first, confining myself to an area some five miles in diameter between the crater and the river. Upon both sides of the latter, below where the ship had landed, was a considerable extent of forest. I ventured into this upon several occasions and once, just about time for us to return to the ship, I came upon a well marked trail in the dust of which were the imprints of three-toed feet. Each day I set the extreme limit of time that I would absent myself from the ship with instructions that two of those remaining aboard should set out in search of me and my companion, should we be absent over the specified number of hours. Therefore, I was unable to follow the trail the day upon which I discovered it, since we had scarcely more than enough time to make a brief examination of the tracks if we were to reach the ship within the limit I had allowed.

It chanced that Norton was with me that day and in his quiet way was much excited by our discovery. We were both positive that the tracks had been made by a four-footed animal, something that weighed between two hundred and fifty and three hundred pounds. How recently it had been used we could scarcely estimate, but the trail itself gave every indication of being a very old one. I was sorry that we had no time to pursue the animal which had made the tracks but determined that upon the following day I should do so. We reached the ship and told the others what we had discovered. They were much interested and many and varied were the conjectures as to the nature of the animals whose tracks we had seen.

After Orthis had been released from arrest Norton had asked permission to return to the former's stateroom. I had granted his request and the two had been very much together ever since. I could not understand Norton's apparent friendship for this man, and it almost made me doubt the young ensign. One day I was to learn the secret of this intimacy, but at the time I must confess that it puzzled me considerably and bothered me not a little, for I had taken a great liking to Norton and disliked to see him so much in the company of a man of Orthis' character.

Each of the men had now accompanied me on my short excursions of exploration with the exception of Orthis. Inasmuch as his parole had fully reinstated him among us in theory at least, I could not very well discriminate against him and leave him alone of all the others aboard ship as I pursued my investigations of the surrounding country.

The day following our discovery of the trail, I accordingly invited him to accompany me, and we set out early, each armed with a revolver and a rifle. I advised West, who automatically took command of the ship during my absence, that we might be gone considerably longer than usual and that he was to feel no apprehension and send out no relief party unless we should be gone a full twenty-four hours, as I wished to follow up the spoor we had discovered, learn where the trail led and have a look at the animal that had made it.

I led the way directly to the spot at which we had found the trail, about four miles down river from the ship and apparently in the heart of dense forest.

The flying-toads darted from tree to tree about us, uttering their weird and plaintive cries, while upon several occasions, as in the past, we saw four-legged snakes such as we had seen upon the day of our landing. Neither the toads nor the snakes bothered us, seeming only to wish to avoid us.

Just before we came upon the trail, both Orthis and I thought we heard the sound of footsteps ahead of us—something similar to that made by a galloping animal—and when we came upon the trail a moment later it was apparent to both of us that dust was hanging in the air and slowly settling on the vegetation nearby. Something, therefore, had passed over the trail but a minute or two before we arrived. A brief examination of the spoor revealed the fact that it had been made by a three-toed animal whose direction of travel was to our right and toward the river, at this point some half mile from us.

I could not help but feel considerable inward excitement, and I was sorry that one of the others had not been with me, for I never felt perfectly at ease with Orthis. I had done considerable hunting in various parts of the world where wild game still exists but I had never experienced such a thrill as I did at the moment that I undertook to stalk this unknown beast upon an unknown trail in an unknown world. Where the trail would lead me, what I should find upon it, I never knew from one step to another, and the lure of it because of that was tremendous. The fact that there were almost nine million square miles of this world for me to explore, and that no Earth Man had ever before set foot upon an inch of it, helped a great deal to compensate for the fact that I knew I could never return to my own Earth again.

The trail led to the edge of the river which at this point was very wide and shallow. Upon the opposite shore, I could see the trail again directly opposite and I knew therefore that this was a ford. Without hesitating, I stepped into the river, and as I did so I glanced to my left to see stretching before me as far as my eye could reach a vast expanse of water. Here then I had stumbled upon the mouth of the river and, beyond, a lunar sea.

The land upon the opposite side of the river was rolling and grass-covered, but in so far as I could see, almost treeless. As I turned my eyes from the sea back toward the opposite shore, I saw that which caused me to halt in my tracks, cock my rifle and issue a cautious warning to Orthis for silence, for there before us upon a knoll stood a small horse-like animal.

It would have been a long shot, possibly five hundred yards, and I should have preferred to have come closer but there was no chance to do that now, for we were in the middle of the river in plain view of the animal which stood there watching us intently. I had scarcely raised my rifle, however, ere it wheeled and disappeared over the edge of the knoll upon which it had been standing.

"What did it look like to you, Orthis?" I asked my companion.

"It was a good ways off," he replied, "and I only just got my binoculars on it as it disappeared, but I could have sworn that it wore a harness of some sort. It was about the size of a small pony, I should say, but it didn't have a pony's head."

"It appeared tailless to me," I remarked.

"I saw no tail," said Orthis, "nor any ears or horns. It was a devilish funny looking thing. I don't understand it. There was something about it —" he paused. "My God, sir, there was something about it that looked human."

"It gave me that same impression, too, Orthis, and I doubt if I should have fired had I been able to cover it, for just at the instant that I threw my rifle to my shoulder I felt that same strange impression that you mention. There was something human about the thing."

As we talked, we had been moving on across the ford which we found an excellent one, the water at no time coming to our waists while the current was scarcely appreciable. Finally, we stepped out on the opposite shore and a moment later, far to the left, we caught another glimpse of the creature that we had previously seen. It stood upon a distant knoll, evidently watching us.

Orthis and I raised our binoculars to our eyes almost simultaneously and for a full minute we examined the thing as it stood there, neither of us speaking, and then we dropped our glasses and looked at each other.

"What do you make of it, sir?" he asked.

I shook my head. "I don't know what to make of it, Orthis," I replied; "but I should swear that I was looking straight into a human face, and yet the body was that of a quadruped."

"There can be no doubt of it, sir," he replied, "and this time one could see the harness and the clothing quite plainly. It appears to have some sort of a weapon hanging at its left side. Did you notice it, sir?"

"Yes, I noticed it, but I don't understand it."

A moment longer we stood watching the creature until it turned and galloped off, disappearing behind the knoll on which it had stood. We decided to follow the trail which led in a southerly direction, feeling reasonably assured that we were more likely to come in contact with the creature or others similar to it upon the trail than off of it. We had gone but a short distance when the trail approached the river again, which puzzled me at the time somewhat, as we had gone apparently directly away from the river since we had left the ford, but after we had gone some mile and a half, we found the explanation, since we came again to another ford while on beyond we saw the river emptying into the sea and realized that we had crossed an island lying in the mouth of the river.

I was hesitating as to whether to make the crossing and continue along the trail or to go back and search the island for the strange creature we had discovered. I rather hoped to capture it, but since I had finally descried its human face, I had given up all intention of shooting it unless I found that it would be necessary to do so in self defense. As I stood there, rather undecided, our attention was attracted back to the island by a slight noise, and as we looked in the direction of the disturbance, we saw five of the creatures eyeing us from high land a quarter of a mile away. When they saw that they were discovered they galloped boldly toward us.

They had come a short distance only, when they stopped again upon a high knoll, and then one of them raised his face toward the sky and emitted a series of piercing howls. Then they came on again toward us nor did they pause until they were within fifty feet of us, when they came to a sudden halt.

Captured

OUR first view of the creatures proved beyond a question of a doubt that they were in effect human quadrupeds. The faces were very broad, much broader than any human faces that I have ever seen, but their profiles were singularly like those of the ancient North American Indians. Their bodies were covered with a garment with short legs that ended above the knees, and which was ornamented about the collar and also about the bottom of each leg with a rather fanciful geometric design. About the barrel of each was a surcingle and connected with it by a backstrap was something analogous to a breeching in Earth horse harness. Where the breeching straps crossed on either side, was a small circular ornament, and there was a strap resembling a trace leading from this forward to the collar, passing beneath a quite large, circular ornament, which appeared to be supported by the surcingle. Smaller straps, running from these two ornaments upon the left side, supported a sheath in which was carried what appeared to be a knife of some description. And upon the right side a short spear was carried in a boot, similarly suspended from the two ornaments, much as the carbine of our ancient Earth cavalry was carried. The spear, which was about six feet long, was of peculiar design, having a slender, well-shaped head, from the base of which a crescent-shaped arm curved backward from one side, while upon the side opposite the crescent was a short, sharp point at right angles to the median line of the weapon.

For a moment we stood there eyeing each other, and from their appearance I judged that they were as much interested in us as we were in them. I noticed that they kept looking beyond us, across the river toward the mainland. Presently, I turned for a glance in the same direction, and far away beyond a thin forest I saw a cloud of dust which seemed to be moving rapidly toward us. I called Orthis' attention to it.

"Reinforcements," I said. "That is what that fellow was calling for when he screamed. I think we had better try conclusions with the five before any more arrive. We will try to make friends first, but if we are unsuccessful we must fight our way back toward the ship at once."

Accordingly, I stepped forward toward the five with a smile upon my lips and my hand outstretched. I knew of no other way in which to carry to them an assurance of our friendliness. At the same time, I spoke a few words in English in a pleasant and conciliatory tone. Although I knew that my words would be meaningless to them, I hoped that they would catch their intent from my inflection.

Immediately upon my advance, one of the creatures turned and spoke to another, indicating to us for the first time that they possessed a spoken language. Then he turned and addressed me in a tongue that was, of course, utterly meaningless to me; but if he had misinterpreted my action, I could not misunderstand that which accompanied his words, for he reared up on his hind feet and simultaneously drew his spear and a wicked-looking, short-bladed sword or dagger, his companions at the same time following his example, until I found myself confronted by an array of weapons backed by scowling, malignant faces. Their leader uttered a single word which I interpreted as meaning halt, and so I halted.

I pointed to Orthis and to myself, and then to the trail along which we had come, and then back in the direction of the ship. I was attempting to tell them that we wished to go back whence we had come. Then I turned to Orthis.

"Draw your revolver," I said, "and follow me. If they interfere we shall have to shoot them. We must get out of this before the others arrive."

As we turned to retrace our steps along the trail, the five dropped upon all fours, still holding their weapons in their fore-paws, and galloped quickly to a position blocking our way.

"Stand aside," I yelled, and fired my pistol above their heads. From their actions, I judged that they had never before heard the report of a firearm, for they stood an instant in evident surprise, and then wheeled and galloped off for about a hundred yards, where they turned and halted again, facing us. They were still directly across our trail, and Orthis and I moved forward determinedly toward them. They were talking among themselves, and at the same time watching us closely.

When we had arrived at a few yards from them, I again threatened them with my pistol, but they stood their ground, evidently reassured by the fact that the thing that I held in my hand, though it made a loud noise, inflicted no injury. I did not want to shoot one of them if I could possibly avoid it, so I kept on toward them, hoping that they would make way for us; but instead they reared again upon their hind feet and threatened us with their weapons.

The Moon Maid

Just how formidable their weapons were, I could not, of course, determine; but I conjectured that if they were at all adept in its use, their spear might be a very formidable thing indeed. I was within a few feet of them now, and their attitude was more war-like than ever, convincing me that they had no intention of permitting us to pass peacefully.

Their features, which I could now see distinctly, were hard, fierce, and cruel in the extreme. Their leader seemed to be addressing me, but, of course, I could not understand him; but when, at last, standing there upon his hind feet, with evidently as much ease as I stood upon my two legs, he carried his spear back in a particularly menacing movement, I realized that I must act and act quickly.

I think the fellow was just on the point of launching his spear at me, when I fired. The bullet struck him square between the eyes, and he dropped like a log, without a sound. Instantly, the others wheeled again and galloped away, this time evincing speed that was almost appalling, clearing spaces of a hundred feet in a single bound, even though handicapped, as they must have been, by the weapons which they clutched in their fore-paws.

A glance behind me showed the dust-cloud rapidly approaching the river, upon the mainland, and calling to Orthis to follow me, I ran rapidly along the trail which led back in the direction of the ship.

The four Moon creatures retreated for about half a mile, and then halted and faced us. They were still directly in our line of retreat, and there they stood for a moment, evidently discussing their plans. We were nearing them rapidly, for we had discovered that we, too, could show remarkable speed, when retarded by gravity only one-sixth of that of Earth. To clear forty feet at a jump was nothing, our greatest difficulty lying in a tendency to leap to too great heights, which naturally resulted in cutting down our horizontal distance. As we neared the four, who had taken their stand upon the summit of a knoll, I heard a great splashing in the river behind us, and turning, saw that their reinforcements were crossing the ford, and would soon be upon us. There appeared to be fully a hundred of them, and our case looked hopeless indeed, unless we could manage to pass the four ahead of us, and reach the comparative safety of the forest beyond the first ford.

"Commence firing, Orthis," I said. "Shoot to kill. Take the two at the left as your targets, and I'll fire at the two at the right. We had better halt and take careful aim, as we can't afford to waste ammunition."

We came to a stop about twenty-five yards from the foremost creature, which is a long pistol shot; but they were standing still upon the crest of a knoll, distinctly outlined against the sky, and were such a size as to present a most excellent target. Our shots rang out simultaneously. The creature at the left, at which Orthis had aimed, leaped high into the air, and fell to the ground, where it lay kicking convulsively. The one at the right uttered a piercing shriek, clutched at its breast, and dropped dead. Then Orthis and I charged the remaining two, while behind us we heard loud weird cries and the pounding of galloping feet. The two before us did not retreat this time, but came to meet us, and again we halted and fired. This time they were so close that we could not miss them, and the last of our original lunar foemen lay dead before us.

We ran then, ran as neither of us had imagined human beings ever could run. I know that I covered over fifty feet in many a leap, but by comparison with the speed of the things behind us, we might have been standing still. They fairly flew over the lavender sward, indicating that those, which we had first seen, had at no time extended themselves in an effort to escape us. I venture to say that some of them leaped fully three hundred feet at a time, and now, at every bound, they emitted fierce and terrible yells, which I assumed to be their war cry, intended to intimidate us.

"It's no use, Orthis," I said to my companion. "We might as well make our stand here and fight it out. We cannot reach the ford. They are too fast for us."

We stopped then, and faced them, and when they saw we were going to make a stand, they circled and halted about a hundred yards distant, entirely surrounding us. We had killed five of their fellows, and I knew we could hope for no quarter. We were evidently confronted by a race of fierce and warlike creatures, the appearance of which, at least, gave no indication of the finer characteristics that are so much revered among humankind upon Earth. After a good look at one of them, I could not imagine the creature harboring even the slightest conception of the word mercy, and I knew that if we ever escaped that fierce cordon, it would be by fighting our way through it.

"Come," I said to Orthis, "straight through for the ford," and turning again in that direction, I started blazing away with my pistol as I walked slowly along the trail. Orthis was at my side, and he, too, fired as rapidly as I. Each time our weapons spoke, a Moon Man fell. And now, they commenced to circle us at a run, much as the savage Indians of the western plains circled the parked wagon trains of our long-gone ancestors in North America. They hurled spears at us, but I think the sound of our revolvers and the effect of the shots had to some measure unnerved them, for their aim was poor and we were not, at any time, seriously menaced.

As we advanced slowly, firing, we made many hits, but I was horrified to see that every time one of the creatures fell, the nearest of his companions leaped upon him and cut his throat from ear to ear. Some of them had only to fall to be dispatched by his fellows. A bullet from Orthis' weapon shattered the hind leg of one of them, bringing him to the ground. It was, of course, not a fatal wound, but the creature had scarcely gone down, when the nearest to him sprang forward, and finished him. And thus we walked slowly toward the ford, and I commenced to have hope that we might reach it and make our escape. If our antagonists had been less fearless, I should have been certain of it, but they seemed almost indifferent to their danger, evidently counting upon their speed to give them immunity from our bullets. I can assure you that they presented most difficult targets, moving as they did in great leaps and bounds. It was probably more their number than our accuracy that permitted us the hits we made.

We were almost at the ford when the circle suddenly broke, and then formed a straight line parallel to us, the leader swinging his spear about his head, grasping the handle at its extreme end. The weapon moved at great speed, in an almost horizontal plane. I was wondering at the purpose of his action, when I saw that three or four of those directly in the rear of him had commenced to swing their spears in a similar manner. There was something strangely menacing about it that filled me with alarm. I fired at the leader and missed, and at the report of my pistol, a half dozen of them let go of their swift whirling spears, and an instant later, I realized the purpose of their strange maneuver; for the heavy weapons shot toward us, butts first, with the speed of lightning, the crescent-like hooks catching us around a leg, an arm and the neck, hurling us backward to the ground, and each time we essayed to rise, we were struck again, until we finally lay there, bruised and half stunned, and wholly at the mercy of our antagonists, who galloped forward quickly, stripping our weapons from us. Those who had hurled their spears at us recovered them, and then they all gathered about, examining us, and jabbering among themselves,

Presently, the leader spoke to me, prodding me with the sharp point of his spear. I took it that he wanted me to arise, and I tried to do so, but I was pretty much all in and fell back each time I essayed to obey. Then he spoke to two of his followers, who lifted me and laid me across the back of a third. There I was fastened in a most uncomfortable position by means of leather straps which were taken from various parts of the harnesses of several of the creatures. Orthis was similarly lashed to another of them, whereupon they moved slowly back in the direction from which they had come, stopping, as they went, to collect the bodies of their dead, which were strapped to the backs of others of their companions. The fellow upon whom I rode had several well-defined gaits, one of which, a square trot, was the acme of torture for me, since I was bruised and hurt and had been placed across him face down, upon my belly; but inasmuch as this gait must have been hard, too, upon him, while thus saddled with a burden, he used it but little, for which I was tremendously thankful. When he changed to a single-foot, which, fortunately for me, he often did, I was much less uncomfortable.

As we crossed the ford toward the mainland, it was with difficulty that I kept from being drowned, since my head dragged in the water for a considerable distance and I was mighty glad when we came out again on shore. The thing that bore me was consistently inconsiderate of me, bumping me against others, and against the bodies of their slain that were strapped to the backs of his fellows. He was apparently quite tireless, as were the others, and we often moved for what seemed many miles at a fast run. Of course, my lunar weight was equivalent to only about thirty pounds on Earth while our captors seemed fully as well-muscled as a small earthly horse, and as we later learned, were capable of carrying heavy burdens.

How long we were on the march, I do not know, for where it is always daylight and there is no sun nor other means of measuring time, one may only guess at its duration, the result being influenced considerably by one's mental and physical sensations during the period. Judged by these considerations, then, we might have been on the trail for many hours, for I was not only most uncomfortable in body, but in mind as well. However that may be, I know only that it was a terrible journey; that we crossed rivers twice after reaching the mainland, and came at last to our destination, amid low hills, where there was a level, park-like space, dotted with weird trees. Here the straps were loosened, and we were dumped upon the ground, more dead than alive, and immediately surrounded by great numbers of creatures who were identical with those who had captured us.

When I was finally able to sit up and look about, I saw that we were at the threshold of a camp or village, consisting of a number of rectangular huts, with high-peaked roofs, thatched or rather shingled, with the broad, round leaves of the trees that grew about.

The Moon Maid

We saw now for the first time the females and the young. The former were similar to the males, except that they were of lighter build, and they were far more numerous. They had udders, with from four to six teats, and many of them were followed by numerous progeny, several that I saw having as high as six young in a litter. The young were naked, but the females wore a garment similar to that worn by the males, except that it was less ornate, as was their harness and other trappings. From the way the women and children rushed upon us as we were unloaded in camp, I felt that they were going to tear us to pieces, and I really believe they would have had not our captors prevented it. Evidently the word was passed that we were not to be injured, for after the first rush they contented themselves with examining us, and sometimes feeling of us or our clothing, the while they discussed us, but with the bodies of those who were slain, it was different, for when they discovered these where they had been unloaded upon the ground, they fell upon them and commenced to devour them, the warriors joining them in the gruesome and terrible feast. Orthis and I understood now that they had cut the throats of their fellows to let the blood, in anticipation of the repast to come.

As we came to understand them and the conditions under which they lived, many things concerning them were explained. For example, at least two-thirds of the young that are born are males, and yet there are only about one-sixth as many adult males, as there are females. They are naturally carnivorous, but with the exception of one other creature upon which they prey, there is no animal in that part of the interior lunar world with which I am familiar, that they may eat with safety. The flying-toad and the walking snake and the other reptilia are poisonous, and they dare not eat them. The time had been, I later learned, possibly, however, ages before, when many other animals roamed the surface of the inner Moon, but all had become extinct except our captors and another creature, of which we, at the time of our capture, knew nothing, and these two preyed upon one another, while the species which was represented by those into whose hands we had fallen, raided the tribes and villages of their own kind for food, and ate their own dead, as we had already seen. As it was the females to whom they must look for the production of animal food, they did not kill these of their own species and never ate the body of one. Enemy women of their own kind, whom they captured, they brought to their villages, each warrior adding to his herd the individuals that he captured. As only the males are warriors, and as no one will eat the flesh of a female, the mortality among the males is, accordingly, extremely high, accounting for the vastly greater number of adult females. The latter are very well treated, as the position of a male in a community is dependent largely upon the size of his herd.

The principal mortality among the females results from three causes—raids by the other flesh-eating species which inhabit the inner lunar world, quarrels arising from jealousy among themselves, and death while bringing forth their young, especially during lean seasons when their warriors have been defeated in battle and have been unable to furnish them with flesh.

These creatures eat fruit and herbs and nuts as well as meat, but they do not thrive well upon these things exclusively. Their existence, therefore, is dependent upon the valor and ferocity of their males whose lives are spent in making raids and forays against neighboring tribes and in defending their own villages against invaders.

As Orthis and I sat watching the disgusting orgy of cannibalism about us, the leader of the party that had captured us came toward us from the center of the village, and speaking a single word, which I later learned meant "come," he prodded us with his spear point until finally we staggered to our feet. Repeating the word, then, he started back into the village.

"I guess he wants us to follow him, Orthis," I said. And so we fell in behind the creature, which was evidently what he desired, for he nodded his head, and stepped on in the direction that he had taken, which led toward a very large hut—by far the largest in the village.

In the side of the hut presented to us there seemed to be but a single opening, a large door covered by heavy hangings, which our conductor thrust aside as we entered the interior with him. We found ourselves in a large room, without any other opening whatsoever, save the doorway through which we had entered, and over which the hanging had again been drawn, yet the interior was quite light, though not so much so as outside, but there were no means for artificial lighting apparent. The walls were covered with weapons and with the skulls and other bones of creatures similar to our captors, though Orthis and I both noticed a few skulls much narrower than the others and which, from their appearance, might have been the human skulls of Earth Men, though in discussing it later, we came to the conclusion that they were the skulls of the females and the young of the species, whose faces are not so wide as the adult male.

Lying upon a bed of grasses at the opposite side of the room was a large male whose skin was of so much deeper lavender hue than the others that we had seen, as to almost suggest a purple. The face, though badly disfigured by scars, and grim and ferocious in the extreme, was an intelligent one, and the instant that I looked into those eyes, I knew that we were in the presence of a leader. Nor was I wrong, for this was the chief or king of the tribe into whose clutches Fate had thrown us.

A few words passed between the two, and then the chief arose and came toward us. He examined us very critically, our clothing seeming to interest him tremendously. He tried to talk with us, evidently asking us questions, and seemed very much disgusted when it became apparent to him that we could not understand him, nor he us, for Orthis and I spoke to one another several times, and once or twice addressed him. He gave some instructions to the fellow who had brought us, and we were taken out again, and to another hut, to which there was presently brought a portion of the carcass of one of the creatures we had killed before we were captured. I could not eat any of it, however, and neither could Orthis; and after a while, by signs and gestures, we made them understand that we wished some other kind of food, with the result that a little later, they brought us fruit and vegetables, which were more palatable and, as we were to discover later, sufficiently nutritious to carry us along and maintain our strength.

I had become thirsty, and by simulating drinking, I finally succeeded in making plain to them my desire in that direction, with the result that they led us out to a little stream which ran through the village, and there we quenched our thirst.

We were still very weak and sore from the manhandling we had received, but we were both delighted to discover that we were not seriously injured, nor were any of our bones broken.

Out of the Storm

SHORTLY after we arrived at the village, they took away our watches, our pocket-knives, and everything that we possessed of a similar nature, and which they considered as curiosities. The chief wore Orthis' wristwatch above one fore-paw and mine above the other, but as he did not know how to wind them, nor the purpose for which they were intended, they did him or us no good. The result was, however, that it was now entirely impossible for us to measure time in any way, and I do not know, even to this day, how long we were in this strange village. We ate when we were hungry, and slept when we were tired. It was always daylight; and it seemed that there were always raiding parties going out or returning, so that flesh was plentiful, and we became rather reconciled to our fate, in so far as the immediate danger of being eaten was concerned, but why they kept us alive, as we had slain so many of their fellows, I could not understand.

It must have been immediately after we arrived that they made an attempt to teach us their language. Two females were detailed for this duty. We were given unlimited freedom within certain bounds, which were well indicated by the several sentries which constantly watched from the summit of hills surrounding the village. Past these we could not go, nor do I know that we had any particular desire to do so, since we realized only too well that there would be little chance of our regaining the ship should we escape the village, inasmuch as we had not the remotest idea in what direction it lay.

Our one hope lay in learning their language, and then utilizing our knowledge in acquiring some definite information as to the surrounding country and the location of the Barsoom.

It did not seem to take us very long to learn their tongue, though, of course, I realize that it may really have been months. Almost before we knew it, we were conversing freely with our captors. When I say freely, it is possible that I exaggerate a trifle, for though we could understand them fairly well, it was with difficulty that we made ourselves understood, yet we managed it some way, handicapped as we were by the peculiarities of the most remarkable language of which I have any knowledge.

It is a very difficult language to speak, and as a written language, would be practically impossible. For example, there is their word gu-e-ho, for which Orthis and I discovered twenty-seven separate and distinct meanings, and that there are others I have little or no doubt. Their speech is more aptly described as song, the meaning of each syllable being governed by the note in which it is sung. They speak in five notes, which we may describe as A, B, C, D and E. Gu sung in A means something radically different from gu sung in E, and again if gu is sung in A, followed by e in C, it means something other than if gu had been sung in D followed by e in A.

Fortunately for us, there are no words of over three syllables, and most of them consist of only one or two, or we should have been entirely lost. The resulting speech, however, is extremely beautiful, and Orthis used to say that if he closed his eyes, he could imagine himself living constantly in grand opera.

The chief's name, as we learned, was Ga-va-go; the name of the tribe or village was

No-vans, while the race to which they belonged was known as Va-gas.

When I felt that I had mastered the language sufficiently well to make myself at least partially understood, I asked to speak to Ga-va-go, and shortly thereafter, I was taken to him.

"You have learned our speech?" he asked.

I nodded in the affirmative. "I have," I said, "and I have come to ask why we are held captives and what you intend to do with us. We did not come to seek a quarrel with you. We wish only to be friends, and to be allowed to go our way in peace."

"What manner of creature are you," he asked, "and where do you come from?"

I asked him if he had ever heard of the Sun or the stars or the other planets or any worlds outside his own, and he replied that he had not, and that there were no such things.

"But there are, Ga-va-go," I said, "and I and my companion are from another world, far, far outside your own. An accident brought us here. Give us back our weapons, and let us go."

He shook his head negatively.

"Where you come from, do you eat one another?" he asked.

"No," I replied, "we do not."

"Why?" he asked, and I saw his eyes narrow as he awaited my reply.

Was it mental telepathy or just luck that put the right answer in my mouth, for somehow, intuitively, I seemed to grasp what was in the creature's mind.

"Our flesh is poison," I said, "those who eat it die."

He looked at me then for a long time, with an expression upon his face which I could not interpret. It may have been that he doubted my word, or again, it may have been that my reply confirmed his suspicion, I do not know; but presently he asked me another question.

"Are there many like you in the land where you live?"

"Millions upon millions," I replied.

"And what do they eat?"

"They eat fruits and vegetables and the flesh of animals," I answered.

"What animals?" he asked.

"I have seen no animals here like them," I replied, "but there are many kinds unlike us, so that we do not have to eat flesh of our own race."

"Then you have all the flesh that you want?"

"All that we can eat," I replied. "We raise these animals for their flesh."

"Where is your country?" he demanded. "Take me to it."

I smiled. "I cannot take you to it," I said. "It is upon another world."

It was quite evident that he did not believe me, for he scowled at me ferociously. "Do you wish to die?" he demanded.

I told him that I had no such longing.

"Then you will lead me to your country," he said, "where there is plenty of flesh for everyone. You may think about it until I send for you again. Go!" And thus he dismissed me. Then he sent for Orthis, but what Orthis told him, I never knew exactly, for he would not tell me, and as our relations, even in our captivity, were far from friendly, I did not urge him to any confidences. I had occasion to notice, however, that from that time Ga-va-go indicated a marked preference for Orthis, and the latter was often called to his hut.

I was momentarily expecting to be summoned in to Ga-va-go's presence, and learn my fate, when he discovered that I could not lead him to my country, where flesh was so plentiful. But at about this time we broke camp, and in the press of other matters, he evidently neglected to take any further immediate action in my case, or at least, so I thought, until I later had reason to suspect that he felt that he need no longer depend upon me to lead him to this land of milk and honey.

The Va-gas are a nomadic race, moving hither and thither, either as they are pressed by some foes, or till their victories have frightened away the other tribes from their vicinity, in either of which events, they march in search of fresh territory. The move that we made now was necessitated by the fact that all the other tribes nearby had fled before the ferocity of the No-vans, whose repeated and successful raids had depleted the villages of their neighbors and filled them with terror.

The breaking of camp was a wonderfully simple operation. All their few belongings, consisting of extra clothing, trappings, weapons, and their treasured skulls and bones of victims, were strapped to the backs of the women. Orthis and I each bestrode a warrior detailed by Ga-va-go for the purpose of transporting us, and we filed out of the village, leaving the huts behind.

Ga-va-go, with a half-dozen warriors, galloped far ahead. Then came a strong detachment of warriors, with the women folks behind them, another detachment of warriors following in the rear of the women and children, while others rode upon either flank. A mile or so in the rear, came three warriors, and there were two or three scattered far out on either flank. Thus we moved, thoroughly protected against surprise, regulating our speed by that of the point with which Ga-va-go traveled.

Because of the women and the children, we moved more slowly than warriors do when on the march alone, when they seldom, if ever, travel slower than a trot, and more generally, at a fast gallop. We moved along a well-worn trail, passing several deserted villages, from which the prey of the No-vans had fled. We crossed many rivers, for the lunar world is well watered. We skirted several lakes, and at one point of high ground, I saw, far at our left, the waters of what appeared to be a great ocean.

There was never a time when Orthis and I were not plentifully supplied with food, for there is an abundance of it growing throughout all the territory we crossed, but the No-vans had been without flesh for several days and were, in consequence, mad with hunger, as the fruits and vegetables which they ate seemed not to satisfy them at all.

We were moving along at a brisk trot when, without warning, we were struck by a sudden gust of wind that swept, cold and refreshing, down from some icy mountain fastness. The effect upon the No-vans was electrical. I would not have had to understand their language to realize that they were terrified. They looked apprehensively about and increased their speed as though endeavoring to overtake Ga-va-go, who was now far ahead with the point. A moment later a dash of rain struck us, and then it was every man for himself and the devil take the hindmost, as they broke into a wild stampede to place themselves close to their chief. Their hysterical flight was like the terrorized rush of wild cattle. They jostled and tripped one another, and stumbled and fell and were trampled upon, in their haste to escape.

Old Ga-va-go had stopped with his point, and was waiting for us. Those who accompanied him seemed equally terrified with the rest, but evidently they did not dare run until Ga-va-go gave the word. I think, however, that they all felt safer when they were close to him, for they had a great deal of confidence in him, yet they were still pretty badly frightened, and it would not have taken much to have set them off again into another rout. Ga-va-go waited until the last of the rearguard straggled in, and then he set off directly toward the mountains, the entire tribe moving in a compact mass, though they might have fallen easy prey to an ambush or any sudden attack. They knew, however, what I half guessed, that knowing that their enemies were as terrified of the storm as they, there was little danger of their being attacked—none whatever, in fact.

We came at last to a hillside covered with great trees which offered some protection from both the wind and the rain, which had now arisen to the proportion of a hurricane.

As we came to a halt, I slipped from the back of the warrior who had been carrying me, and found myself beside one of the women who had taught Orthis and me the language of the Va-gas.

"Why is everyone so terrified?" I asked her.

"It is Zo-al," she whispered, fearfully. "He is angry."

"Who is Zo-al?" I asked.

She looked at me in wide-eyed astonishment. "Who is Zo-al!" she repeated. "They told me that you said that you came from another world, and I can well believe it, when you ask, who is Zo-al?"

"Well, who is he?" I insisted.

"He is a great beast," she whispered. "He is everywhere. He lives in all the great holes in the ground, and when he is angry, he comes forth and makes the water fall and the air run away. We know that there is no water up there," and she pointed toward the sky. "But when Zo-al is angry, he makes water fall from where there is no water, so mighty is Zo-al, and he makes the air to run away so that the trees fall before it as it rushes past, and huts are knocked flat or carried high above the ground. And then, O terror of terrors, he makes a great noise, before which mighty warriors fall upon the ground and cover up their ears. We have angered Zo-al, and he is punishing us, and I do not dare to ask him not to send the big noise."

It was at that instant that there broke upon my ears the most terrific detonation that I have ever heard. So terrific was it that I thought my ear drums had burst, and simultaneously, a great ball of fire seemed to come rolling down from the mountain heights above us.

The woman, covering her ears, shuddered, and when she saw the ball of fire, she voiced a piercing shriek.

"The light that devours!" she cried. "When that comes too, it is the end, for then is Zo-al mad with rage."

The ground shook to the terrifying noise, and though the ball of fire did not pass close to us, still could I feel the heat of it even as it went by at a distance, leaving a trail of blackened and smoking vegetation in its rear. What flames there were, the torrential rain extinguished almost immediately. It must have traveled about ten miles, down toward the sea, across rolling hills and level valleys, when suddenly it burst, the explosion being followed by a report infinitely louder than that which I had first heard. An earthquake could scarce have agitated the ground more terrifyingly than did this peal of lunar thunder.

I had witnessed my first lunar electrical storm, and I did not wonder that the inhabitants of this strange world were terrified by it. They attribute these storms, as they do all their troubles, to Zo-al, a great beast, which is supposed to dwell in the depth of the lunar craters, the lower ends of which open into the interior lunar world. As we cowered there among the trees, I wondered if they were not afraid that the wind would blow the forest down and crush them, and I asked the woman who stood beside me.

"Yes," she said, "that often happens, but more often does it happen that if one is caught in a clearing, the air that runs away picks him up and carries him along to drop him from a great height upon the hard ground. The trees bend before they break, and those who watch are warned, and they escape destruction if they are quick. When the wind that runs seizes one, there is no escape."

"It seems to me," I said, "that it would have been safer if Ga-va-go had led us into one of those sheltered ravines," and I indicated a gorge in the hillside at our right. "No," she said, "Ga-va-go is wise. He led us to the safest spot. We are sheltered from the air that runs away, and perhaps a little from the light that devours, nor can the waters that drown, reach us here, for presently they will fill that ravine full."

Nor was she wrong. Rushing down from the hillside, the water poured in torrents into the ravine, and presently, though it must have been twenty or thirty feet deep, it was filled almost to overflowing. Whoever had sought refuge there, would have been drowned and washed away to the big ocean far below. It was evident that Ga-va-go had not been actuated solely by blind terror, though I came to know that he must have felt terror, for these terrible electrical storms alone can engender it in the breasts of these fearless and ferocious people.

The storm must have lasted for a considerable time; how long, of course, I do not know, but some idea of its duration may be gained by the fact that I became hungry and ate of the fruit of the trees, which sheltered us, at least six times, and slept twice. We were soaked to the skin and very cold, for the rain evidently came from a great altitude. During the entire storm, the No-vans scarcely moved from their positions beneath the trees, with their backs toward the storm, where they stood with lowered heads like cattle. We experienced twelve detonations of the ground-shaking thunder, and witnessed six manifestations of the light that devours.

Trees had fallen all about us, and as far as we could see, the grasses lay flat and matted upon the ground. They told me that storms of the severity of this were infrequent, though rain and wind, accompanied by electrical manifestations, might be expected at any season of the year—I use that expression from habit, for one can scarcely say that there are any well-marked seasonal changes within the Moon that could indicate corresponding divisions of time as upon the Earth. From what I was able to gather from observation and from questioning the Va-gas, lunar vegetation reproduces itself entirely independent of any seasonal restrictions, the frequency and temperature of the rains having, seemingly, the greatest influence in the matter. A period of drought and cold rains retards growth and germination, while frequent warm rains have an opposite effect, the result being that you find vegetation of the same variety in all stages of development, growing side by side—blossoms upon one tree, fruit upon another, and the dry seed-pods upon a third. Not even, therefore, by the growth of plant life, might one measure time within the Moon, and the period of gestation among the Va-gas is similarly irregular, being affected by the physical condition of the female as well as by climatic conditions, I imagine. When the tribe is well-fed, and the weather warm, the warriors victorious, and the minds of the women at peace, they bring forth their young in an incredibly short period. On the other hand, a period of cold, or of hunger, and of long marches, following defeat, induces an opposite result. It seems to me that the females nurse their young for a very short period of time, for they grow rapidly, and as soon as their molars are through, and they can commence eating meat, they are weaned. They are devilish little rascals, their youthful exuberance finding its outlet in acts of fiendish cruelty. As they are not strong enough to inflict their tortures on adults they perpetrate them upon one another, with the result that the weaker are often killed, after they are weaned and have left the protection of their savage mothers. Of course, they tried to play some of their fiendish tricks on Orthis and myself, but after we had knocked a few of them down, they left us severely alone.

During the storm, they huddled, shivering and cold, against the adults. Possibly I should be ashamed to say it, but I felt no pity for them, and rather prayed that they would all be chilled to death, so hateful and wantonly cruel were they. As they become adults, they are less wanton in their atrocities, though no less cruel, their energies, however, being intelligently directed upon the two vital interests of their lives—procuring flesh and women.

Shortly after the rain ceased, the wind began to abate, and as I was cold, cramped and uncomfortable, I walked out into the open, in search of exercise that would stimulate my circulation and warm me again. As I walked briskly to and fro, looking here and there at the evidences of the recent storm, my glance chanced to rise toward the sky, and there I saw what appeared at first to be a huge bird, a few hundred feet above the forest in which we had sought shelter. It was flapping its great wings weakly and seemed to be almost upon the verge of exhaustion, and though I could see that it was attempting to fly back in the direction of the mountains, the force of the wind was steadily carrying it in the direction of the lowlands and the sea. Presently it would be directly above me, and as it drew nearer, I knit my brows in puzzlement, for except for its wings, and what appeared to be a large hump upon its back, its form bore a striking resemblance to that of a human being.

Some of the No-vans evidently saw me looking upwards thus interestedly, and prompted by curiosity, joined me. When they saw the creature flying weakly overhead, they set up a great noise, until presently all the tribe had run into the open and were looking up at the thing above us.

The wind was lessening rapidly, but it still was strong enough to carry the creature gently toward us, and at the same time I perceived that whatever it was, it was falling slowly to the ground, or more correctly, sinking slowly.

"What is it?" I asked of the warrior standing beside me.

"It is a U-ga," he replied. "Now shall we eat."

I had seen no birds in the lunar world, and as I knew they would not eat the flying reptiles, I guessed that this must be some species of bird life, but as it dropped closer, I became more and more convinced that it was a winged human being, or at least a winged creature with human form.

As it fluttered toward the ground, the No-vans ran along to meet it, waiting for it to fall within reach. As they did so, Ga-va-go called to them to bring the creature to him alive and unharmed.

I was about a hundred yards from the spot, when the poor thing finally fell into their clutches. They dragged it to the ground roughly, and a moment later I was horrified to see them tear its wings from it and the hump from its back. There was a great deal of grumbling at Ga-va-go's order, as following the storm and their long fast, the tribe was ravenously hungry.

"Flesh, flesh!" they growled. "We are hungry. Give us flesh!" But Ga-va-go paid no attention to them, standing to one side beneath a tree, awaiting the prisoner that they were bringing toward him.

The Moon Maid

ORTHIS, who was becoming the almost constant companion of the chief, was standing beside the latter, while I was twenty-five or thirty yards away, and directly between Ga-va-go and the warriors who were approaching with the prisoner, who would of necessity have to pass close beside me. I remained where I was, therefore, in order to get a better look at it, which was rather difficult because it was almost entirely surrounded by No-vans. However as they came opposite me, there was a little break momentarily in the ranks, and I had my first opportunity, though brief, for a closer observation of the captive; and my comprehension was almost staggered by what my eyes revealed to me, for there before me, was as perfectly formed a human female as I had ever seen. By earthly standards, she appeared a girl of about eighteen, with hair of glossy blackness, that suggested more the raven's wing than aught else and a skin of almost marble whiteness, slightly tinged with a creamy shade. Only in the color of her skin, did she differ from earthly women in appearance, except that she seemed far more beautiful than they. Such perfection of features seemed almost unbelievable. Had I seen her first posed motionless, I could have sworn that she was chiseled from marble, yet there was nothing cold about her appearance. She fairly radiated life and feeling. If my first impression had been startling, it was nothing to the effect that was produced when she turned her eyes full upon me. Her black brows were two thin, penciled arches, beneath which were dark wells of light, vying in blackness with her raven hair. On either cheek was just the faintest suggestion of a deeper cream, and to think that these hideous creatures saw in that form divine only flesh to eat! I shuddered at the thought and then my eyes met hers and I saw an expression of incredulity and surprise registered in those liquid orbs. She half-turned her head as she was dragged past, that she might have a further look at me, for doubtless she was as surprised to see a creature like me as I was to see her.

Involuntarily I started forward. Whether there was an appeal for succor in those eyes I do not know, but at least they aroused within me instantly, that natural instinct of a human male to protect the weak. And so it was that I was a little behind her and to her right, when she was halted before Ga-va-go.

The savage Va-gas' chieftain eyed her coldly, while from all sides there arose cries of "Give us flesh! Give us flesh! We are hungry!" to which Ga-va-go paid not the slightest attention.

"From whence come you, U-ga?" he demanded.

Her head was high, and she eyed him with cold dignity as she replied, "From Laythe."

The No-van raised his brows. "Ah," he breathed, "from Laythe. The flesh of the women from Laythe is good," and he licked his thin lips.

The girl narrowed her eyes, and tilted her chin a bit higher. "Rympth!" she ejaculated, disgustedly.

As rympth is the name of the four-legged snake of Va-nah, the inner lunar world, and considered the lowest and most disgusting of created things, she could not well have applied a more opprobrious epithet to the No-van chieftain, but if it had been her intent to affront him, his expression gave no indication that she had succeeded.

"Your name?" he asked.

"Nah-ee-lah," she replied.

"Nah-ee-lah," he repeated, "Ah, you are the daughter of Sagroth, Jemadar of Laythe."

She nodded in indifferent affirmation, as though aught he might say was a matter of perfect indifference to her.

"What do you expect us to do with you?" asked Ga-va-go, a question which suggested a cat playing with a mouse before destroying it.

"What can I expect of the Va-gas, other than that they will kill me and eat me?" she replied.

A roar of savage assent arose from the creatures surrounding her. Ga-va-go flashed a quick look of anger and displeasure at his people.

"Do not be too sure of that," he snapped. "This be little more than a meal for Ga-va-go alone. It would but whet the appetite of the tribe."

"There are two more," suggested a bold warrior, close beside me, pointing at me and at Orthis.

"Silence!" roared Ga-va-go. "Since when did you become chief of the No-vans?"

"We can starve without a chief," muttered the warrior who had spoken, and from two or three about him arose grumblings of assent.

Swift, at that, Ga-va-go reared upon his hind feet, and in the same motion, drew and buried his spear, the sharp point penetrating the breast of the malcontent, piercing his heart. As the creature fell, the warrior closest to him slit his throat, while another withdrew Ga-va-go's spear from the corpse, and returned it to the chief.

"Divide the carcass among you," commanded the chief, "and whosoever thinks that there is not enough, let him speak as that one spoke, and there shall be more flesh to eat."

Thus did Ga-va-go, chief of the No-vans, hold the obedience of his savage tribesmen. There was no more muttering then, but I saw several cast hungry eyes at me—hungry, angry eyes that boded me no good.

In what seemed an incredibly short space of time, the carcass of the slain warrior had been divided and devoured, and once again we set out upon the march, in search of new fields to conquer, and fresh flesh to eat.

Now Ga-va-go sent scouts far in advance of the point, for we were entering territory which he had not invaded for a long time, a truth which was evidenced by the fact that there were only about twenty warriors in the tribe, besides Ga-va-go, who were at all familiar with the territory. Naturally quarrelsome and disagreeable, the No-vans were far from pleasant companions upon that memorable march, since they had not recovered from the fright and discomforts of the storm and, in addition, were ravenously hungry. I imagine that none, other than Ga-va-go, could have held them. What his purpose was in preserving the three prisoners, that would have made such excellent food for the tribe, I did not know. However, we were not slain, though I judged the fellow who carried me, would much sooner have eaten me, and to vent his spite upon me he trotted as much as he could, and I can assure you that he had the most devilishly execrable trot I ever sat. I felt that he was rather running the thing into the ground, for he had an easy rack, which would have made it much more comfortable for both of us, and inasmuch as I knew that I was safe as long as I was under Ga-va-go's protection, I made up my mind to teach the fellow a lesson, which I finally did, although almost as much to my discomfort as his, by making no effort to ease myself upon his back so that at every step I rose high and came down hard upon him, sitting as far back as possible so as to pound his kidneys painfully. It made him very angry and be threatened me with all kinds of things if I didn't desist, but I only answered by suggesting that he take an easier gait, which at last he was forced to do.

Orthis was riding ahead with Ga-va-go, who as usual led the point, while the new prisoner astride a No-van warrior was with the main body, as was I.

Once the warriors that we bestrode paced side by side, and I saw the girl eyeing me questioningly. She seemed much interested in the remnants of my uniform, which must have differed greatly from any clothing she had seen in her own world. It seemed that she spoke and understood the same language that Ga-va-go used, and so at last I made bold to address her.

"It is unfortunate," I said, "that you have fallen into the hands of these creatures. I wish that I might be of service to you, but I also am a prisoner."

She acknowledged my speech with a slight inclination of her head, and at first I thought that she was not going to reply, but finally looking me full in the face she asked, "What are you?"

"I am one of the inhabitants of the planet Earth."

"Where is that, and what is planet?" she asked, for I had had to use the Earth word, since there is no word of similar meaning in the language of the Va-gas.

"You know, of course," I said, "that space outside of Va-nah is filled with other worlds. The closest to Va-nah is Earth, which is many, many times larger than your world. It is from Earth that I come."

She shook her head. "I do not understand," she said. She closed her eyes, and waved her hands with a gesture that might have included the universe. "All, all is rock," she said, "except here in the center of everything, in this space we call Va-nah. All else is rock."

I suppressed a smile at the vast egotism of Va-nah, but yet how little different is it from many worldlings, who conceive that the entire cosmos exists solely for the inhabitants of Earth. I even know men in our own enlightened twenty-first century, who insist that Mars is not inhabited and that the messages that are purported to come from our sister planet, are either the evidences of a great world hoax, or the voice of the devil luring people from belief in the true God.

"Did you ever see my like in Va-nah?" I asked her.

"No," she replied, "I never did, but I have not been to every part of Va-nah. Va-nah is a very great world, and there are many corners of it of which I know nothing."

"I am not of Va-nah," I told her again, "I am from another world far, far away;" and then I tried to explain something of the universe to her— of the sun and the planets and their satellites, but I saw that it was as far beyond her as are the conceptions of eternity and space beyond the finite mind of Earth Men. She simply couldn't get it, that was all. To her, everything was solid rock that we know as space. She thought for a long time, though, and then she said, "Ah, perhaps after all there may be other worlds than Va-nah. The great Hoos, those vast holes that lead into the eternal rock, may open into other worlds like Va-nah. I have heard that theory discussed, but no one in Va-nah believes it. It is true, then!" she exclaimed brightly, "and you come from another world like Va-nah. You came through one of the Hoos, did you not?"

"Yes, I came through one of the Hoos," I replied—the word means hole in the Va-gas tongue—"but I did not come from a world like Va-nah. Here you live upon the inside of a hollow sphere. We Earth Men live upon the outside of a similar though much larger sphere."

"But what holds it up?" she cried, laughing. It was the first time that she had laughed, and it was a very contagious laugh, and altogether delightful. Although I knew that it would probably be useless, I tried to explain the whole thing to her, commencing with the nebular hypothesis, and winding up with the relations that exist between the Moon and the Earth. If I didn't accomplish anything else, I at least gave her something to distract her mind from her grave predicament, and to amuse her temporarily, for she laughed often at some of my statements. I had never seen so gay and vivacious a creature, nor one so entirely beautiful as she. The single, sleeveless, tunic-like garment that she wore, fell scarcely to her knees and as she bestrode the No-van warrior, it often flew back until her thighs, even, were exposed. Her figure was divinely perfect, its graceful contours being rather accentuated than hidden by the diaphanous material of her dainty covering; but when she laughed, she exposed two rows of even white teeth that would be the envy of the most beautiful of Earth Maids.

"Suppose," she said, "that I should take a handful of gravel and throw it up in the air. According to your theory the smaller would all commence to revolve about the larger and they would go flying thus wildly around in the air forever, but that is not what would happen. If I threw a handful of gravel into the air it would fall immediately to the ground again, and if the worlds you tell me of were cast thus into the air, they too would fall, just as the gravel falls."

It was useless, but I had known that from the beginning. What would be more interesting would be to question her, and that I had wished to do for some time, but she always put me off with a pretty gesture and a shake of her head, insisting that I answer some of her questions instead, but this time I insisted.

"Tell me, please," I asked, "how you came to the spot where you were captured, how you flew, and what became of your wings, and why, when they tore them from you, it did not injure you?"

She laughed at that quite merrily.

"The wings do not grow upon us," she explained, "we make them and fasten them upon our arms."

"Then you can support yourself in the air with wings fastened to your arms?" I demanded, incredulously.

"Oh, no," she said, "the wings we use simply for propelling ourselves through the air. In a bag, upon our backs, we carry a gas that is lighter than air. It is this gas which supports us, and we carry it in such quantities as to maintain a perfect equilibrium, so that we may float at any altitude, or with our wings rise or fall gently; but as I hovered over Laythe, came the air that runs, and seizing me with its strong arms bore me off across the surface of Va-nah. Futilely I fought against it until I was spent and weak, and then it dropped me into the clutches of the Va-gas, for the gas in my bag had become depleted. It was not intended to carry me aloft for any great length of time."

She had used a word which, when I questioned her, she explained so that I understood that it meant time, and I asked her what she meant by it and how she could measure it, since I had seen no indication of the Va-gas having any conception of a measurable aspect of duration.

Nah-ee-lah explained to me that the Va-gas, who were a lower order, had no means of measuring time, but that the U-ga, the race to which she belonged, had always been able to compute time through their observation of the fact that during certain periods the bottoms of the hoos, or craters, were illuminated, and for another period they were dark, and so they took as a unit of measure the total period from the beginning of this light in a certain crater to its beginning again, and this they called a ula, which corresponds with a sidereal month. By mechanical means they divide this into a hundred parts, called ola, the duration of each of which is about six hours and thirty-two minutes earth time. Ten ulas make a keld, which one might call the lunar year of about two hundred and seventy-two days earth time.

I asked her many questions and took great pleasure in her answers, for she was a bright, intelligent girl, and although I saw many evidences of regal dignity about her, yet her manner toward me was most natural and unaffected, and I could not help but feel that she occupied a position of importance among her own people.

Our conversation was suddenly interrupted, however, by a messenger from the point, who came racing back at tremendous speed, carrying word from Ga-va-go that the scouts were signaling that they had discovered a large village, and that the warriors were to prepare to fight.

Immediately we moved up rapidly to Ga-va-go, and then we all advanced toward the scout who could be seen upon a knoll far ahead. We were cautioned to silence, and as we moved at a brisk canter over the soft, pale lavender vegetation of the inner Moon, the feet of the Va-gas giving forth no sound, the picture presented to my earthly eyes was weird and mysterious in the extreme.

When we reached the scout, we learned that the village was situated just beyond a low ridge not far distant, so Ga-va-go gave orders that the women, the children, and the three prisoners should remain under a small guard where we were until they had topped the ridge, when we were to advance to a position where we might overlook the village, and if the battle was against the No-vans we could retreat to a point which he indicated to the warriors left to guard us. This was to be the rendezvous, for following defeat the Va-gas warriors scatter in all directions, thus preventing any considerable body of them being attacked and destroyed by a larger body of the pursuing enemy.

As we stood there upon the knoll, watching Ga-va-go and his savage warriors galloping swiftly toward the distant ridge, I could not but wonder that the inhabitants of the village which they were about to attack had not placed sentinels along the ridge to prevent just such a surprise as this, but when I questioned one of the warriors who had been left to guard us, he said that not all the Va-gas tribes were accustomed to posting sentinels when they felt themselves reasonably safe from attack. It had always been Ga-va-go's custom, however, and to it they attributed his supremacy among the other Va-gas tribes over a large territory.

"After a tribe has made a few successful raids and returned victorious, they are filled with pride," the warrior explained to me, "and presently they begin to think that no one dares to attack them and then they grow careless, and little by little the custom of posting sentinels drops into disuse. The very fact that they have no sentinels indicates that they are a large, powerful and successful tribe. We shall feed well for a long time."

The very idea of the thought that was passing through his mind, was repellent in the extreme, and I fairly shuddered when I contemplated the callousness with which this creature spoke of the coming orgy, in which he hoped to devour flesh of his own kind.

The Moon Maid

Presently we saw our force disappear beyond the ridge, and then we too, advanced, and as we moved forward there came suddenly to us, from the distance the fierce and savage war cry of the No-vans and a moment later it was answered by another no less terrible, rising from the village beyond the ridge. Our guards hastened us then, to greater speed, until, at a full run, we mounted the steep slope of the ridge and halted upon its crest.

Below us lay a broad valley, and in the center a long, beautiful lake, the opposite shore of which was clothed in forest while that nearest us was open and park-like, dotted here and there with beautiful trees, and in this open space we descried a large village.

The ferocity of the scene below us was almost indescribable. The No-vans warriors were circling the village at a rapid run, attempting to keep the enemy in a compact mass within, where it would present a better target for their spears. Already the ground was dotted with corpses. There were no wounded, for whenever one fell the nearest to him whether friend or foe cut his throat, since the victors would devour them all without partiality. The females and the young had taken refuge in the huts, from the doorways of which they watched the progress of the battle. The defenders attempted repeatedly to break through the circling No-vans. The warrior with whom I had been talking told me that if they were successful the females and the young would follow them through the break scattering in all directions, while their warriors attempted to encircle the No-vans. It was almost immediately evident that the advantage lay with the force that succeeded in placing this swift-moving circle about its enemy, and keeping the enemy within it until they had been dispatched, for those in the racing circle presented a poor target, while the compact mass of warriors milling in the center could scarce be missed.

Following several unsuccessful attempts to break through the ring of savage foemen the defenders suddenly formed another smaller ring within, and moving in the opposite direction to the No-vans, raced in a rapid circle. No longer did they cast spears at the enemy, but contented themselves with leaping and bounding at a rapid gait. At first it seemed to me that they had lost their heads with terror, but at last I realized that they were executing a strategic maneuver which demonstrated both cunning and high discipline. In the earlier stages of the battle each side had depended for its weapons upon those hurled by the opposing force, but now the defenders hurled no weapons, and it became apparent that the No-vans would soon no longer have spears to cast at them. The defenders were also lessening their casualties by moving in a rapid circle in a direction opposite to that taken by the attackers, but it must have required high courage and considerable discipline to achieve this result since it is difficult in the extreme to compel men to present themselves continuously as living targets for a foe while they themselves are permitted to inflict no injury upon the enemy.

Ga-va-go apparently was familiar with the ruse, for suddenly he gave a loud cry which was evidently a command. Instantaneously, his entire force wheeled in their tracks and raced in the opposite direction paralleling the defenders of the village, and immediately thereafter cast their remaining spears at comparatively easy targets.

The defenders, who were of the tribe called Lu-thans, wheeled instantly to reverse the direction of their flight. Those wounded in the sudden onslaught stumbled and fell, tripping and impeding the others, with the result that for an instant they were a tangled mass, without order or formation. Then it was that Ga-va-go and his No-vans leaped in upon them with their short, wicked sword-daggers. At once the battle resolved itself into a ferocious and bloody hand-to-hand conflict, in which daggers and teeth and three-toed paws each did their share to inflict injury upon an antagonist. In their efforts to escape a blow, or to place themselves in an advantageous position, many of the combatants leaped high into the air, sometimes between thirty and forty feet. Their shrieks and howls were continuous and piercing. Corpses lay piled so thick as to impede the movements of the warriors, and the ground was slippery with blood, yet on and on they fought, until it seemed that not a single one would be left alive.

"It is almost over," remarked the warrior at my side. "See, there are two or three No-vans now attacking each Lu-than."

It was true, and I saw that the battle could last but a short time. As a matter of fact it ended almost immediately, the remaining Lu-thans suddenly attempting to break away and scatter in different directions. Some of them succeeded in escaping, possibly twenty but I am sure that there were not more than that, and the rest fell.

Ga-va-go and his warriors did not pursue the few who had escaped, evidently considering that it was not worth the effort, since there were not enough of them to menace the village, and there was already plenty of meat lying fresh and warm upon the ground.

We were summoned now, and as we filed down into the village, great was the rejoicing of our females and young.

Guards were placed over the women and children of the defeated Lu-thans, and then at a signal from Ga-va-go, the No-vans fell upon the spoils of war. It was a revolting spectacle, as mothers devoured their sons, and wives, their husbands. I do not care to dwell upon it.

When the victors had eaten their fill, the prisoners were brought forth under heavy guard, and divided by the Va-gas between the surviving No-vans warriors. There was no favoritism shown in the distribution of the prisoners, except that Ga-va-go was given first choice, and received also those that remained after as nearly equal a distribution as possible had been made. I had expected that the male children would be killed, but they were not, being inducted into the tribe upon an equal footing with those that had been born into it.

Being capable of no sentiments of either affection or loyalty, it is immaterial to these creatures to what tribe they belong, but once inducted into a tribe, the instinct of self-preservation holds them to it, since they would be immediately slain by the members of any other tribe.

I learned shortly after this engagement that Ga-va-go had lost fully half his warriors, and that this was one of the most important battles that the tribe had ever fought. The spoils, however, had been rich, for they had taken over ten thousand women and fully fifty thousand young, and great quantities of weapons, harness, and apparel.

The flesh that they could not eat was wrapped up and buried, and I was told that it would remain in excellent condition almost indefinitely.

A Fight and a Chance

AFTER occupying the new village, Orthis and I were separated, he being assigned a hut close to Ga-va-go, while I was placed in another section of the village. If I could have been said to have been on good terms with any of the terrible creatures of the tribe, it was with the woman who had taught me the language of the Va-gas, and it was from her that I learned why Orthis was treated with such marked distinction by Ga-va-go, whom, it seemed, he had promised to lead to the land of our origin, where, he had assured the savage chieftain, he would find flesh in abundance.

Nah-ee-lah was confined in still another part of the village, and I only saw her occasionally, for it was evident that Ga-va-go wished to keep the prisoners separated. Upon one occasion when I met her at the shore of the lake I asked her why it was that they had not slain and eaten her, and she told me that when Ga-va-go had discovered her identity, and that her father was a Jemadar, a ruler of a great city, he had sent messengers with an offer to return Nah-ee-lah for a ransom of one hundred young women of the city of Laythe.

"Do you think your father will send the ransom?" I asked.

"I do not know," she replied. "I do not see how they are going to get a message to him, for ordinarily, my race kills the Va-gas on sight. They may succeed, however, but even so, it is possible that my father will not send the ransom. I would not wish him to. The daughters of my father's people are as dear to them, as am I to him. It would be wrong to give a hundred of the daughters of Laythe in return for one, even though she be the daughter of the Jemadar."

We had drunk, and were returning toward our huts when, wishing to prolong our conversation and to be with this pleasant companion while I might, I suggested that we walk farther into the woods and gather fruit. Nah-ee-lah signified her willingness, and together we strolled out of the village into the denser woods at its rear, where we found a particularly delicious fruit growing in abundance. I gathered some and offered it to her, but she refused, thanking me, saying that she had but just eaten.

"Do they bring the fruit to you," I asked, "or do you have to come and gather it yourself?"

"What fruit I get I gather," she replied, "but they bring me flesh. It is of that which I have just eaten, and so I do not care for fruit now."

"Flesh!" I exclaimed. "What kind of flesh?"

"The flesh of the Va-gas, of course," she replied. "What other flesh might a U-ga eat?"

I fear that I ill-concealed my surprise and disgust at the thought that the beautiful Nah-ee-lah ate of the flesh of the Va-gas.

"You, too, eat of the flesh of these creatures?" I demanded.

"Why not?" she asked. "You eat flesh, do you not, in your own country. You have told me that you raise beasts solely for their flesh."

"Yes," I replied, "that is true, but we eat only the flesh of lower orders; we do not eat the flesh of humans."

"You mean that you do not eat the flesh of your own species," she said.

"Yes," I replied, "that is what I mean."

"Neither do I," she said. "The Va-gas are not of the same species as the U-ga. They are a lower order, just as are the creatures whose flesh you eat in your own country.

The Moon Maid

You have told me of beef, and of mutton, and of pork, which you have described as creatures that run about on four legs, like the Va-gas. What is the difference, then, between the eating of the flesh of pork and beef or mutton, and the eating of Va-gas, who are low creatures also?"

"But they have human faces!" I cried, "and a spoken language."

"You had better learn to eat them," she said, "otherwise you will eat no flesh in Va-nah."

The more I thought about it the more reason I saw in her point of view. She was right. She was no more transgressing any natural law in eating the flesh of the Va-gas than do we, eating the flesh of cattle. To her the Va-gas were less than cattle. They were dangerous and hated enemies. The more I analyzed the thing, the more it seemed to me that we humans of the earth were more surely transgressing a natural law by devouring our domestic animals, many of which we learned to love, than were the U-ga of Va-nah in devouring the flesh of their four-footed foes, the Va-gas. Upon our earthly farms we raise calves and sheep and little pigs, and oftentimes we become greatly attached to individuals and they to us. We gain their confidence, and they have implicit trust in us, and yet, when they are of the right age, we slay and devour them. Presently it did not seem either wrong or unnatural that Nah-ee-lah should eat the flesh of the Va-gas, but as for myself, I could never do it, nor ever did.

We had left the forest, and were returning to the village to our huts when, near the large hut occupied by Ga-va-go, we came suddenly upon Orthis. At the sight of us together he scowled.

"If I were you," he said to me, "I would not associate with her too much. It may arouse the displeasure of Ga-va-go."

It was the first time that Orthis had spoken to me since we had occupied this village. I did not like his tone or his manner.

"You will please to mind your own business, Orthis," I said to him, and continued on with Nah-ee-lah. I saw the man's eyes narrow malignantly, and then he turned, and entered the hut of Ga-va-go, the chief of the No-vans.

Every time I went to the river, I had to pass in the vicinity of Nah-ee-lah's hut. It was a little out of my way, but I always made the slight detour in the hope of meeting her, though I had never entered her hut nor called for her, since she had never invited me and realizing her position, I did not wish to intrude. I was of course ignorant of the social customs of her people, and feared offending her accidentally.

It chanced that the next time that I walked down to the lake shore, following our stroll in the woods, I made my usual detour that I might pass by the hut of Nah-ee-lah. As I came near I heard voices, one of which I recognized as that of Nah-ee-lah, and the other, a man's voice. The girl's tones were angry and imperious.

"Leave my presence, creature!" were the first words that I could distinguish, and then the man's voice.

"Come," he said, ingratiatingly. "Let us be friends. Come to my hut, and you will be safe, for Ga-va-go is my friend." The voice was the voice of Orthis.

"Go!" she ordered him again. "I would as soon lie with Ga-va-go as with you."

"Know then," cried Orthis, angrily, "that you will go, whether you wish it or not, for Ga-va-go has given you to me. Come!" and then he must have seized her, for I heard her cry out, "How dare you lay hands upon me, Nah-ee-lah, princess of Laythe!"

I was close beside the entrance to the hut now, and I did not wait to hear any more, but thrusting the hanging aside entered. There they were, in the center of the single room, Orthis struggling to drag the girl toward the opening while she resisted and struck at him. Orthis' back was toward me and he did not know that there was another in the hut until I had stepped up behind him and grasping him roughly by the shoulder, had jerked him from the girl and swung him about facing me.

"You cad," I said, "get out of here before I kick you out, and don't ever let me hear of you molesting this girl again."

His eyes narrowed, and he looked at me with an ugly light in them. "Since boyhood, you have cheated me out of all I wished. You ruined my life on Earth, but now, conditions are reversed. The tables are turned. Believe me, then, when I tell you that if you interfere with me you sign your own death warrant. It is only by my favor that you live at all. If I gave the word Ga-va-go would destroy you at once. Go then to your hut and stop your meddling in the affairs of others—a habit that you developed in a most flagrant degree on Earth, but which will avail you nothing here within the Moon. The woman is mine. Ga-va-go has given her to me. Even if her father should fail to send the ransom her life shall be spared as long as I desire her. Your interference then can only result in your death, and do her no good, for provided you are successful in keeping me from her, you would be but condemning her to death in the event that her father does not send the ransom, and Ga-va-go has told me that there is little likelihood of that, since it is scarcely possible that his messengers will be able to deliver Ga-va-go's demands to Sagroth."

"You have heard him," I said, turning to the girl. "What are your wishes in the matter. Perhaps he speaks the truth."

"I have no doubt but that he speaks the truth," she replied, "but know, strangers, that the honor of a princess of Laythe is dearer than her life."

"Very well, Orthis," I said to the man. "You have heard her. Now get out."

He was almost white with anger, and for a moment I thought that he was going to attack me, but he was ever a coward, and contenting himself with giving me a venomous look, he walked from the hut without another word.

I turned to Nah-ee-lah, after the hanging had dropped behind Orthis. "It is too bad," I said, "that with all your suffering at the hands of the Va-gas, you should also be annoyed by one who is practically of your own species."

"Your kindness more than compensates," she replied graciously. "You are a brave man, and I am afraid that you are going to suffer for your protection of me. This man is powerful. He has made wonderful promises to Ga-va-go. He is going to teach him how to use the strange weapons that you brought from your own world. The woman who brings me my meat told me of all this, and that the tribe is much excited by the promises that your friend has made to Ga-va-go. He will teach them to make the weapons, such as you slew their warriors with, so that they will be invincible, and may go abroad in Va-nah slaying all who oppose them and even raiding the cities of the U-ga. He has told them that he will lead them to the strange thing which brought you from your world to Va-nah, and that there they will find other weapons, like those that you carried, and having the noise which they make, and the things with which they kill. All these he says they may have, and that later he will build other things, such as brought you from your world to Va-nah, and he will take Ga-va-go and all the No-vans to what you call Earth."

"If there is any man in the universe who might do it, it is he," I replied, "but there is little likelihood that he can do it. He is merely deceiving Ga-va-go in the hope of prolonging his own life, against the possibility that an opportunity to escape will develop, in which event he will return to our ship and our friends. He is a bad man though, Nah-ee-lah, and you must be careful of him. There is a vacant hut near yours, and I will come and live in it. There is no use in asking Ga-va-go, for if he is friendly with Orthis, he will not permit me to make the change. If you ever need me, call 'Julian' as loud as you can, and I will come."

"You are very good," she said. "You are like the better men of Laythe, the high nobles of the court of the Jemadar, Sagroth, my father. They too are honorable men, to whom a woman may look for protection, but there are no others in all Va-nah since the Kalkars arose thousands of kelds ago, and destroyed the power of the nobles and the Jemadars, and all the civilization that was Va-nah's. Only in Laythe, have we preserved a semblance of the old order. I wish I might take you to Laythe, for there you would be safe and happy. You are a brave man. It is strange that you are not married."

I was upon the point of making some reply, when the hangings at the doorway parted, and a No-van warrior entered. Behind him were three others. They were walking erect, with drawn spears.

"Here he is," said the leader, and then, addressing me, "Come!"

"Why?" I asked. "What do you want of me?"

"Is it for you to question," he demanded, "when Ga-va-go commands?"

"He has sent for me?" I asked.

"Come!" repeated the leader, and an instant later they had hooked their spears about my arms and neck and none too gently they dragged me from the hut. I had something of a presentiment that this was to be the end. At the doorway I half turned to glance back at the girl. She was standing wide-eyed and tense, watching them drag me away.

"Good-bye—Julian," she said. "We shall never meet again for there is none to carry our souls to a new incarnation."

"We are not dead yet," I called back, "and remember if you need me call me," and then the hanging dropped behind us, and she was shut off from my vision.

They did not take me to my own hut, but to another, not far distant from Nah-ee-lah's, and there they bound my hands and feet with strips of leather and threw me upon the ground. Afterwards they left me, dropping the hanging before the entrance. I did not think that they would eat me, for Orthis had joined with me in explaining to Ga-va-go and the others that our flesh was poisonous, and though they may have questioned the veracity of our statements, nevertheless I was quite sure that they would not risk the chance of our having told the truth.

The Va-gas obtain their leather by curing the hides of their dead. The better portions they use for their trappings and harness. The other portions they cut into thin strips, which they use in lieu of rope. Most of this is very strong, but some of it is not, especially that which is improperly cured.

The warriors who had been sent to seize me had scarcely left the hut before I commenced working with my bonds in an attempt to loosen or break them. I exerted all my strength in the effort, until I became sure that those which held my hands were stretching. The effort, however, was very tiring, and I had to stop often and rest. I do not know how long I worked at them, but it must have been a very long time before I became convinced that however much they gave they were not going to break. Just what I intended to do with my freedom I do not know, since there was little or no chance that I might escape from the village. Perpetual daylight has its disadvantages, and this was one of them, that there was no concealing nocturnal darkness during which I might sneak away from the village unseen.

As I lay resting after my exertions, I suddenly became aware of a strange, moaning sound from without, and then the hut shook, and I realized that another storm had come. Soon after I heard the beat of rain drops on the roof, and then a staggering, deafening peal of lunar thunder. As the storm waxed in violence, I could imagine the terror of the No-vans, nor even in my plight could I resist the desire to smile at their discomfiture. I knew that they must all be hiding in their huts, and again I renewed my efforts to break the bonds at my wrists, but all to no avail; and then suddenly, above the moaning of the wind and the beating of the rain, there came distinctly to my ears in a clear, full voice, a single word: "Julian!"

"Nah-ee-lah," I thought. "She needs me. What are they doing to her?" There flashed quickly before my mental vision a dozen scenes, in each of which I saw the divine figure of the Moon Maid, the victim of some fiendish brutality. Now she was being devoured by Ga-va-go; now some of the females were tearing her to pieces, and again the warriors were piercing that beautiful skin with their cruel spears; or it was Orthis, come to claim Ga-va-go's gift. It was this last thought, I think, which turned me almost mad, giving to my muscles the strength of a dozen men. I have always been accounted a powerful man, but in the instant that that sweet voice came across the storm to find me, and my imagination pictured her in the clutches of Orthis, something within moved me to Herculean efforts far transcending aught that I had previously achieved. As though they had been cotton twine now, the leather bonds at my wrists snapped asunder, and an instant later those at my ankles were torn away, and I was upon my feet. I sprang to the door and into the open, where I found myself in a maelstrom of wind and rain. In two bounds I had cleared the space between the hut in which I had been confined and that occupied by Nah-ee-lah, had torn the hanging aside, and had sprung into the interior; and there I beheld the materialization of my last vision—there was Orthis, one arm about the slender body of the girl pinning her arms close to her side, while his other hand was at her throat, choking her and pressing her slowly backward across his knees toward the ground.

He was facing the door this time, and saw me enter, and as he realized who it was, he hurled the girl roughly from him and rose to meet me. For once in his life he seemed to know no fear, and I think that what with his passion for the girl, and the hatred he felt for me, and the rage that my interference must have engendered, he was momentarily insane, for he suddenly leaped upon me like a madman, and for an instant I came near going down beneath his blows—but only for an instant, and then I caught him heavily upon the chin with my left fist, and again, full in the face with my right, and though he was a splendid boxer, he was helpless in my hands. Neither of us had a weapon, or one of us certainly would have been killed in short order. As it was I tried to kill him with my bare fists, and at last, when he had fallen for the dozenth time, and I had picked him up and held him upon his feet and struck him repeatedly again and again, he no longer moved. I was sure that he was dead, and it was with a feeling of relief and of satisfaction in a duty well performed that I looked down upon his lifeless body. Then I turned to Nah-ee-lah.

"Come," I said, "there has been given to us this chance for escape. Never again may such a fortuitous combination of circumstances arise. The Va-gas will be hiding in their huts, crouching in terror of the storm. I do not know whither we may fly, but wherever it be, we can be in no greater danger than we are here."

She shuddered a little at the thought of going out into the terrors of the storm. Though not so fearful of it as the ignorant Va-gas, she still feared the wrath of the elements, as do all the inhabitants of Va-nah, but she did not hesitate, and as I stretched out a hand, she placed one of hers within it, and together we stepped out into the swirling rain and wind.

A Fight with a Tor-ho

NAH-EE-LAH and I passed through the village of the No-vans undetected, since the people of Ga-va-go were cowering in their huts, terror-stricken by the storm. The girl led me immediately to high ground and upward along a barren ridge toward the high mountains in the distance. I could see that she was afraid though she tried to hide it from me, putting on a brave front that I was sure she was far from feeling. My respect for her increased, as I have always respected courage, and I believe that it requires the highest courage to do that which fills one with fear. The man who performs heroic acts without fear is less brave than he who overcomes his cowardice.

Realizing her fear I retained her hand in mine, that the contact might impart to her a little of the confidence that I felt, now that I was temporarily at least out of the clutches of the Va-gas.

We had reached the ridge above the village when the thought that we were weaponless and without means of protection overwhelmed me. I had been in so much of a hurry to escape the village that I had overlooked this very vital consideration. I spoke to Nah-ee-lah about it, telling her that I had best return to the village and make an effort to regain possession of my own weapons and ammunition. She tried to dissuade me, telling me that such an attempt was foredoomed to failure and prophesying that I would be recaptured.

"But we cannot cross this savage world of yours, Nah-ee-lah, without means of protection," I urged. "We do not know at what minute some fierce creature may confront us—think how helpless we shall be without weapons with which to defend ourselves."

"There are only the Va-gas," she said, "to fear in this part of Va-nah. We know no other dangerous beast, except the tor-ho. They are seldom seen. Against the Va-gas your weapons would be useless, as you already have discovered. The risk of meeting a tor-ho is infinitely less than that which you will incur if you attempt to enter Ga-va-go's hut to secure your weapons. You simply could not do it and escape, for doubtless the dwelling of the Chief is crowded with warriors."

I was compelled, finally, to admit the wisdom of her reasoning and to forego an attempt to secure my rifle and pistol, though I can assure you that I felt lost without them, especially when thus venturing forth into a new world so strange to me as Va-nah, and so savage. As a matter of fact, from what I gleaned from Nah-ee-lah, there was but a single spot upon the entire inner lunar world where she and I could hope to be even reasonably free from danger, and that was her native city of Laythe. Even there I should have enemies, she told me, for her race is ever suspicious of strangers; but the friendship of the princess would be my protection, she assured me with a friendly pressure of the hand.

The rain and wind must have persisted for a considerable time, for when it was finally over and we looked back through a clear atmosphere we found that a low range of mountains lay between us and the distant sea. We had crossed these and were upon a plateau at the foot of the higher peaks. The sea looked very far away indeed, and we could not even guess at the location of the No-vans village from which we had escaped.

"Do you think they will pursue us?" I asked her.

"Yes," she said; "they will try to find us, but it will be like looking for a raindrop in the ocean. They are creatures of the low-lands—I am of the mountains. Down there," and she pointed into the valley, "they might find me easily, but in my own mountains—no."

"We are near Laythe?" I asked.

"I do not know. Laythe is hard to find—it is well hidden. It is for this reason that it exists at all. Its founders were pursued by the Kalkars, and had they not found an almost inaccessible spot they would have been discovered and slain long before they could have constructed an impregnable city."

She led me then straight into the mighty mountains of the Moon, past the mouths of huge craters that reached through the lunar crust to the surface of the satellite, along the edges of yawning chasms that dropped three, four, yes, sometimes five miles, sheer into frightful gorges, and then out upon vast plateaus, but ever upward toward the higher peaks that seemed to topple above us in the distance. The craters, as a rule, lay in the deep gorges, but some we found upon the plateaus, and even a few opened into the summits of mountain peaks as do those upon the outer surface of planets. Those in the low places were, I believe, the openings through which the original molten lunar core was vomited forth by the surface volcanoes upon the outer crust.

Nah-ee-lah told me that the secret entrance to Laythe lay just below the lip of one of these craters, and it was this she sought. To me the quest seemed hopeless, for as far as the eye could reach lay naught but an indescribable jumble of jagged peaks, terrific gorges and bottomless craters. Yet always the girl seemed to find a way among or about them— instinctively, apparently, she found trails and footholds where there were no trails and where a chamois might have been hard put to it to find secure footing.

In these higher altitudes we found a vegetation that differed materially from that which grew in the lowlands. Edible fruits and berries were, however, still sufficiently plentiful to keep us reasonably well supplied with food. When we were tired we usually managed to find a cave in which we could rest in comparative security, and when it was possible to do so Nah-ee-lah always insisted upon barricading the entrance with rocks, since there was always the danger, she told me, of our being attacked by tor-hos. These blood-thirsty creatures while rare, were nevertheless very much to be feared, since not only were they voracious meat eaters and of such a savage disposition that they attacked nearly everything they saw in wanton ferocity, but even a minor wound inflicted by their fangs or talons often proved fatal, because of the fact that their principal diet was the poisonous flesh of the rympth and the flying toad: I tried to get Nah-ee-lah to describe the creature to me, but inasmuch as there was no creature with which we were both familiar that she might compare it with, I learned little more from her than that it stood between eighteen inches and two feet in height, had long, sharp fangs, four legs and was hairless.

As an aid to climbing, as well as to give me some means of protection, I broke a stout and rather heavy branch from one of the mountain trees, the wood of which was harder than any that I had seen growing in the lowlands. To roam a strange and savage world armed only with a wooden stick seemed to me the height of rashness, but there was no alternative until the time arrived when I might find the materials with which to fashion more formidable weapons. I had in mind a bow and arrows and was constantly on the lookout for wood which I considered adapted to the former, and I also determined to forego my cane for a spear whenever the material for the making of one came to hand. I had little time, however, for such things, as it seemed that when we were not sleeping we were constantly upon the move, Nah-ee-lah becoming more and more impatient to find her native city as the chances for so doing lessened—and it seemed to me that they were constantly lessening. While I was quite sure that she had no more idea where Laythe lay than I, yet we stumbled on and on and on, through the most stupendous mountain ranges that the mind of man can conceive, nor ever, apparently, did Nah-ee-lah discover a single familiar landmark upon which to hang a shred of hope that eventually we might come upon Laythe.

I never saw such a sanguine and hopeful person as Nah-ee-lah. It was her constant belief that Laythe lay just beyond the next mountain, in spite of the fact that she was invariably mistaken—which seemed never to lessen the exuberance of her enthusiasm for the next guess—which I knew beforehand was going to be a wrong guess.

Once just after we had rounded the shoulder of a mountain we came upon a little strip of level land clinging to the side of a mighty peak. I was in the lead—a position which I tried always to take when it was not absolutely necessary for Nah-ee-lah to go ahead in order to find a trail. As I came around the shoulder of the mountain, and in full sight of the little level area, I was positive that I saw a slight movement among some bushes at my right about halfway along one side of the little plain.

As we came abreast of the spot, upon which I kept my eye, there broke upon our ears the most hideous scream that I have ever heard, and simultaneously there leaped from the concealment of the bushes a creature about the size of a North American mountain lion, though quite evidently a reptile and probably a tor-ho, as such it proved to be. There was something about the head and face which suggested the cat family to me, yet there was really no resemblance between it and any of the earthly felines. It came at me with those terrible curved fangs bared and bristling and as it came it emitted the most terrifying sounds—I have called them screams, because that word more nearly describes them than any other, and yet they were a combination of shrieks and moans—the most blood-curdling that I have ever heard.

Nah-ee-lah grasped my arm. "Run!" she cried, "run." But I shook her loose and stood my ground. I wanted to run, that I will admit, but where to? The creature was covering the ground at tremendous speed and our only avenue of escape was the narrow trail over which we had just come, which clung precariously to the side of a perpendicular cliff. And so I stood there waiting, my feeble stick grasped in both hands. Just what I expected to do with it I scarcely knew until the tor-ho was upon me. Then I swung for its head as a batter swings for a pitched ball. I struck it square upon the nose —a terrific blow that not only stopped it, but felled it. I could hear the bones crushing beneath the impact of my crude weapon and I thought that I had done for the thing with that single blow, but I did not know the tremendous vitality of the creature. Almost instantly it was up and at me again, and again I struck it, this time upon the side of the head, and again I heard bones crush and again it fell heavily to the ground.

What appeared to be cold blood was oozing slowly from its wounded face as it came at me for the third time, its eyes glaring hideously, its broken jaws agape to seize me, while its shrieks and moans rose to a perfect frenzy of rage and pain. It reared up and struck at me with its talons now, but I met it again with my bludgeon and this time I broke a fore leg.

How long I fought that awful thing I cannot even guess. Time and time again it charged me furiously and each time, though often by but a miracle of fortune, I managed to keep it from closing, and each blow that I delivered crushed and maimed it a little more, until at last it was nothing but a bleeding wreck of pulp, still trying to crawl toward me upon its broken legs and seize me and drag me down with its broken, toothless jaws. Even then it was with the greatest difficulty that I killed it, that I might put it out of its misery.

Rather exhausted, I turned to look for Nah-ee-lah, and much to my surprise, I found her standing directly behind me.

"I thought you had run away," I said,

"No," she said, "you did not run and so I did not, but I never thought that you would be able to kill it."

"You thought that it would kill me, then?" I asked.

"Certainly," she replied. "Even now I cannot understand how you were able to overcome a tor-ho with that pitiful little stick of wood."

"But if you thought I was going to be killed," I insisted, "why was it that you did not seek safety in flight?"

"If you had been killed I should not have cared to live," she said simply.

I did not exactly understand her attitude and scarcely knew what reply to make.

"It was very foolish of you," I said at last, rather blunderingly, "and if we are attacked again you must run and save yourself."

She looked at me for a moment with a peculiar expression upon her face which I could not interpret and then turned and resumed her way in the direction in which we had been traveling when our journey had been interrupted by the tor-ho. She did not say anything, but I felt that I had offended her and I was sorry. I did not want her falling in love with me, though, and according to earthly standards, her statement that she would rather die than live without me might naturally have been interpreted as a confession of love. The more I thought of it, however, as we moved along in silence, the more possible it seemed to me that her standards might differ widely from mine and that I was only proving myself to be an egotistical ass in assuming that Nah-ee-lah loved me. I wished that I might explain matters to her, but it is one of those things that is rather difficult to explain, and I realized that it might be made much worse if I attempted to do so.

We had been such good friends and our fellowship had been so perfect that the apparently strained silence which existed between us was most depressing. Nah-ee-lah had always been a talkative little person and always gay and cheerful, even under the most trying conditions.

I was rather tired out after my encounter with the tor-ho and should have liked to stop for a rest, but I did not suggest it, neither did Nah-ee-lah, and so we continued on our seemingly interminable way, though, almost exhausted as I was, I dropped some little distance behind my beautiful guide.

She was quite out of sight ahead of me upon the winding trail when suddenly I heard her calling my name aloud. I answered her as, simultaneously, I broke into a run, for I did not know but that she might be in danger, though her voice did not sound at all like it. She was only a short distance ahead and when I came in sight of her I saw her standing at the edge of a mighty crater. She was facing me and she was smiling.

"Oh, Julian," she cried, "I have found it. I am home and we are safe at last."

"I am glad, Nah-ee-lah," I said. "I have been much worried on account of the dangers to which you have been constantly subjected, as well as because of a growing fear that you would never be able to find Laythe."

"Oh, my!" she exclaimed, "I knew that I would find it. If I had to hunt through every mountain range in Va-nah I would have found it."

"You are quite sure that this is the crater where lies the entrance to Laythe?" I asked her.

"There is no doubt of it, Julian," she replied, and she pointed downward over the lip of the crater toward a narrow ledge which lay some twenty feet below and upon which I saw what appeared to be the mouth of a cave opening into the crater.

"But, how are we going to reach it?" I asked.

"It may be difficult," she replied, "but we will find a way."

"I hope so, Nah-ee-lah," I said, "but without a rope or wings I do not see how we are going to accomplish it."

"In the mouth of the tunnel," explained Nah-ee-lah, "there are long poles, each of which has a hook at one end. Ages ago there were no other means of ingress or egress to the city and those who came out to hunt or for any other purpose came through this long tunnel from the city, and from the ledge below they raised their poles and placed the hooked ends over the rim of the crater, after which it was a simple matter to clamber up or down the poles as they wished; but it has been long since these tunnels were used by the people of Va-nah, who had no further need of them after the perfection of the flying wings which you saw me using when I was captured by the Va-gas."

"If they used poles, so may we," I said, "since there are plenty of young trees growing close to the rim of the crater. The only difficulty will be in felling one of them."

The Moon Maid

"We can do that," said Nah-ee-lah, "if we can find some sharp fragments of stone. It will be slow work, but it can be done," and she started immediately to hunt for a fragment with a cutting edge. I joined her in the search and it was not long before we had discovered several pieces of obsidian with rather sharp edges. We then started to work upon a young tree about four inches in diameter that grew almost straight for a height of some thirty feet.

Cutting the tree down with our bits of lava glass was tedious work, but finally it was accomplished, and we were both much elated when the tree toppled and fell to the ground. Cutting away the branches occupied almost as long a time, but that, too, was finally accomplished. The next problem which confronted us was that of making the top of the pole secure enough to hold while we descended to the ledge before the mouth of the tunnel. We had no rope and nothing with which to fashion one, other than my garments, which I was loth to destroy, inasmuch as in these higher altitudes it was often cold. Presently, however, I hit upon a plan which, if Nah-ee-lah's muscles and my nerves withstood the strain it put upon them, bade fair to assure the success of our undertaking. I lowered the larger end of the pole over the side of the crater until the butt rested upon the ledge before the mouth of the tunnel. Then I turned to Nah-ee-lah.

"Lie down flat at full length, Nah-ee-lah," I directed her, "and hold this pole securely with both hands. You will only have to keep it from toppling to the sides or outward, and to that, I think, your strength is equal. While you hold it, I will descend to the mouth of the tunnel and raise one of the regular hooked poles which you say should be deposited there. If they are not, I believe that I can hold our own pole securely from below while you descend." She looked over into the vast abyss below and shuddered. "I can hold it at the top," she said, "if the bottom does not slip from the ledge."

"That is a chance that I shall have to take," I replied, "but I will descend very carefully and I think there will be little danger upon that score."

I could see, upon a more careful examination of the ledge below, that there was some danger of an accident such as she suggested.

Nah-ee-lah took her position as I had directed and lay grasping the pole securely in both hands at the rim of the crater, which was absolutely perpendicular at this point, and I prepared to make the perilous descent.

I can assure you that my sensations were far from pleasurable as I looked over into that awful abyss. The crater itself was some four or five miles in diameter, and, as

I had every reason to suspect, extended fully two hundred and fifty miles through the lunar crust to the surface of the Moon. It was one of the most impressive moments of my life as I clung balancing upon the edge of that huge orifice, gazing into the silent, mysterious depths below. And then I seized the pole very gently and lowered myself over the edge.

"Courage, Julian!" whispered Nah-ee-lah; "I shall hold very tight."

"I shall be quite safe, Nah-ee-lah," I assured her. "I must be safe, for if I am not, how are you to reach the ledge and Laythe?"

As I descended very slowly I tried not to think at all, but to exclude from my mind every consideration of the appalling depths beneath me. I could not have been more than two feet from the ledge when the very thing that we both tried so hard to guard against transpired—a splintered fragment of the pole's butt crumpled beneath my weight and that slight jar was just sufficient to start the base of my precarious ladder sliding toward the edge of the narrow projection upon which I had rested it, and beyond which lay eternity. Above me I heard a slight scream and then the pole slipped from the ledge and I felt myself falling.

It was over in an instant. My feet struck the ledge and I threw myself within the mouth of the tunnel. And then, above me, I heard Nah-ee-lah's voice crying in agonized tones:

"Julian! Julian! I am falling!"

Instantly I sprang to my feet and peered upward from the mouth of the tunnel upon a sight that froze my blood, so horrifying did it seem, for there above me, still clinging to the pole, hung Nah-ee-lah, her body, with the exception of her legs, completely over the edge of the crater. Just as I looked up she dropped the pole and although I made a grab for it I missed it and it fell past me into the maw of the crater.

"Julian! Julian! You are safe!" she cried; "I am glad of that. It terrified me so when I thought you were falling and I tried my best to hold the pole, but your weight dragged me over the edge of the crater. Good-bye, Julian, I cannot hold on much longer."

"You must, Nah-ee-lah!" I cried; "do not forget the hooked poles that you told me of. I will find one and have you down in no time." And even as I spoke I turned and dove into the tunnel; but my heart stood still at the thought that the poles might not be there. My first glance revealed only the bare rock of walls and floor and ceiling and no hooked poles in sight. I sprang quickly farther into the tunnel which turned abruptly a few yards ahead of me and just around the bend my eyes were gladdened by the sight of a dozen or more of the poles which Nah-ee-lah had described. Seizing one of them, I ran quickly back to the entrance. I was almost afraid to look up, but as I did so I was rewarded by the sight of Nah-ee-lah's face smiling down at me—she could smile even in the face of death, could Nah-ee-lah.

"Just a moment more, Nah-ee-lah!" I cried to her, as I raised the pole and caught the hook upon the crater's rim. There were small protuberances on either side of the pole for its entire length, which made climbing it comparatively simple.

"Make haste, Julian!" she cried, "I am slipping."

It wasn't necessary for her to tell me to make haste. I think that I never did anything more quickly in my life than I climbed that pole, but I reached her not an instant too soon, for even as my arm slipped about her, her hold upon the ledge above gave way, and she came down head foremost upon me. I had no difficulty in catching her and supporting her weight. My only fear was that the hook above might not sustain the added weight under the strain of her falling body. But it held, and I blessed the artisan who had made it thus strong.

A moment later I had descended to the mouth of the tunnel and drawn Nah-ee-lah into the safety of its interior. My arm was still around her and hers about me as she stood there sobbing upon my breast. She was utterly relaxed and her supple body felt so helpless against me that there was suddenly aroused within me a feeling such as I had never experienced before—a rather indescribable feeling, yet one which induced, seemingly, an irresistible and ridiculous desire to go forth and slay whole armies of men in protection of this little Moon Maid. It must have been a sudden mental reversion to some ancient type of crusading ancestor of the Middle Ages —some knight in armor from whose loins I had sprung, transmitting to me his own flamboyant, yet none the less admirable, chivalry. The feeling rather surprised me, for I have always considered myself more or less practical and hard-headed. But more sober thought finally convinced me that it was but a nervous reaction from the thrilling moments through which we had both just passed, coupled with her entire helplessness and dependence upon me. Be that as it may, I disengaged her arms from about my neck as gently and as quickly as I could and lowered her carefully to the floor of the tunnel, so that she sat with her back leaning against one of the walls.

"You are very brave, Julian," she said, "and very strong."

"I am afraid I am not very brave," I told her. "I am almost weak from fright even now—I was so afraid that I would not reach you in time, Nah-ee-lah."

"It is the brave man who is afraid after the danger is past," she said. "He has no time to think of fear until after the happening is all over. You may have been afraid for me, Julian, but you could not have been afraid for yourself, or otherwise you would not have taken the risk of catching me as I fell. Even now I cannot understand how you were able to hold me."

"Perhaps," I reminded her, "I am stronger than the men of Va-nah, for my earthly muscles are accustomed to overcoming a gravity six times as great as that upon your world. Had this same accident happened upon Earth I might not have been able to hold you when you fell."

An Attack by Kalkars

THE tunnel in which I found myself and along which Nah-ee-lah led me toward the city of Laythe was remarkable in several particulars. It was largely of natural origin, seemingly consisting of a series of caves which may have been formed by bubbles in the cooling lava of the original molten flow and which had later been connected by man to form a continuous subterranean corridor. The caves themselves were usually more or less spherical in shape and the debris from the connecting passageways had been utilized to fill the bottoms of them to the level of the main floor of the passageway. The general trend of the tunnel was upward from the point at which we had entered it, and there was a constant draught of air rushing along it in the same direction in which we were moving, assuring me that it was undoubtedly well ventilated for its full length. The walls and ceiling were coated with a substance of which radium was evidently one of the ingredients, since even after we had lost sight of the entrance the passageway was well illuminated. We had been moving along in silence for quite a little distance when I finally addressed Nah-ee-lah.

"It must seem good," I said, "to travel again this familiar tunnel of your native city. I know how happy I should be were I thus approaching my own birthplace."

"I am glad to be returning to Laythe," she said, "for many reasons, but for one I am sorry, and as for this passageway it is scarcely more familiar to me than to you, since I have traversed it but once before in my life and that when I was a little girl and came here with my father and his court upon the occasion of his periodical inspection of the passageway, which is now practically never used."

"If you are not familiar with the tunnel," I asked, "are you sure that there is no danger of our going astray at some fork or branch?"

"There is but the one passageway," she replied, "which leads from the crater to Laythe."

"And how long is the tunnel?" I asked. "Will we soon enter the city?"

"No," she replied, "it is a great distance from the crater to Laythe."

We had covered some little distance at this time, possibly five or six miles, and she had scarcely ceased speaking when a turn in the passageway led us into a cave of larger proportions than any through which we had previously passed and from the opposite side of which two passageways diverged.

"I thought there were no branches," I remarked.

"I do not understand it," she said. "There is no branch from the tunnel of Laythe."

"Could it be possible that we are in the wrong tunnel?" I asked, "and that this does not lead to Laythe?"

"A moment before I should have been sure that we were in the right tunnel," she replied, "but now, Julian, I do not know, for never had I heard of any branch of our own tunnel."

We had crossed the cave and were standing between the openings of the two divergent passageways.

"Which one shall we take?" I asked, but again she shook her head.

"I do not know," she replied.

"Listen!" I cautioned her. "What was that?" For I was sure that I had heard a sound issuing from one of the tunnels.

We stood peering into an aperture which revealed about a hundred yards of the passageway before an abrupt turn hid the continuation of it from our view. We could hear what now resolved itself into the faint sound of voices approaching us along the corridor, and then quite suddenly the figure of a man appeared around the corner of the turn. Nah-ee-lah leaped to one side out of sight, drawing me with her.

"A Kalkar!" she whispered. "Oh, Julian, if they find us we are lost."

"If there is only one of them I can take care of him," I said.

"There will be more than one," she replied; "there will be many."

"Then, let us return the way we came and make our way to the top of the crater's rim before they discover us. We can throw their hooked poles into the crater, including the one which we used to ascend from the mouth of the tunnel, thus effectually preventing any pursuit."

"We cannot cross this room again to the tunnel upon the opposite side without being apprehended," she replied. "Our only hope is in hiding in this other tunnel until they have passed and trusting to chance that we meet no one within it."

"Come, then," I said. "I dislike the idea of flying like a scared rabbit, but neither would there be any great wisdom in facing armed men without a single weapon of defense."

Even as we had whispered thus briefly together, we found the voices from the other tunnel had increased and I thought that I noted a tone of excitement in them, though the speakers were still too far away for us to understand their words. We moved swiftly up the branch tunnel, Nah-ee-lah in the lead, and after passing the first turn we both felt comparatively safe, for Nah-ee-lah was sure that the men who had interrupted our journey were a party of hunters on their way to the outer world by means of the crater through which we had entered the tunnel and that they would not come up the branch in which we were hiding. Thus believing, we halted after we were safely out of sight and hearing of the large cave we had just left.

"That man was a Kalkar," said Nah-ee-lah, "which means that we are in the wrong tunnel and that we must retrace our steps and continue our search for Laythe upon the surface of the ground." Her voice sounded tired and listless, as though hope had suddenly deserted her brave heart. We were standing shoulder to shoulder in the narrow corridor and I could not resist the impulse to place an arm about her and comfort her.

"Do not despair, Nah-ee-lah," I begged her; "we are no worse off than we have been and much better off than before we escaped the Va-gas of Ga-va-go. Then do you not recall that you mentioned one drawback to your return to Laythe—that you might be as well off here as there? What was the reason, Nah-ee-lah?"

"Ko-tah wants me in marriage," she replied. "Ko-tah is very powerful. He expects one day to be Jemadar of Laythe. This he cannot be while I live unless he marries me."

"Do you wish to marry him?" I asked.

"No," she said; "not now. Before—" she hesitated—"before I left Laythe I did not care so very much; but now I know that I cannot wed with Ko-tah."

"And your father," I continued, "what of him—will he insist that you marry Ko-tah?"

The Moon Maid

"He cannot do otherwise," replied Nah-ee-lah, "for Ko-tah is very powerful. If my father refuses to permit me to marry him Ko-tah may overthrow him, and when my father is dead, should I still refuse to marry Ko-tah he may slay me, also, and then become Jemadar easily, for the blood of Jemadars flows in his veins."

"It appears to me, Nah-ee-lah, that you will be about as badly off at home as anywhere else in Va-nah. It is too bad that I cannot take you to my own Earth, where you would be quite safe, and I am sure, happy."

"I wish that you might, Julian," she replied simply.

I was about to reply when she placed slim fingers upon my lips. "Hush, Julian!" she whispered, "they are following us up this corridor. Come quickly, we must escape before they overtake us," and so saying, she turned and ran quickly along the corridor which led neither of us knew whither.

But we were soon to find out, for we had gone but a short distance when we came to the tunnel's end in a large circular chamber, at one end of which was a rostrum upon which were a massive, elaborately carved desk and a chair of similar design. Below the rostrum were arranged other chairs in rows, with a broad aisle down the center. The furniture, though of peculiar design and elaborately carved with strange figures of unearthly beasts and reptiles, was not, for all of that, markedly dissimilar to articles of the same purpose fabricated upon Earth. The chairs had four legs, high backs and broad arms, seeming to have been designed equally for durability, service, and comfort.

I glanced quickly around the apartment, as we first entered, only taking in the details later, but I saw that there was no other opening than the one through which we had entered.

"We will have to wait here, Nah-ee-lah," I said. "Perhaps, though, all will be well—the Kalkars may prove friendly."

She shook her head negatively. "No," she said, "they will not be friendly."

"What will they do to us?" I asked.

"They will make slaves of us," she replied, "and we shall spend the balance of our lives working almost continuously until we drop with fatigue under the cruelest of taskmasters, for the Kalkars hate us of Laythe and will hesitate at nothing that will humiliate or injure us."

She had scarcely ceased speaking when there appeared in the entrance of the cave the figure of a man about my own height dressed in a tunic similar to Nah-ee-lah's but evidently made of leather. He carried a knife slung in a scabbard depending

86

from a shoulder belt, and in his right hand he grasped a slender lance. His eyes were close set upon either side of a prominent, hooked nose. They were watery, fishy, blue eyes, and the hair growing profusely above his low forehead was flaxen in color. His physique was admirable, except for a noticeable stoop. His feet were very large and his gait awkward when he moved. Behind him I could see the heads and shoulders of others. They stood there grinning at us for a moment, most malevolently, it seemed to me, and then they entered the cave—a full dozen of them. There were several types, with eyes and hair of different colors, the former ranging from blue to brown, the latter from light blond to almost black.

As they emerged from the mouth of the tunnel they spread out and advanced slowly toward us. We were cornered like rats in a trap. How I longed for the feel of my automatic at my hip! I envied them their slender spears and their daggers. If I could have but those I might have a chance at least to take Nah-ee-lah out of their clutches and save her from the hideous fate of slavery among the Kalkars, for I had guessed what such slavery would mean to her from the little that she had told me, and I had guessed, too, that she would rather die than submit to it. For my own part, life held little for me; I had long since definitely given up any hope of ever returning to my own world, or of finding the ship and being re-united with West and Jay and Norton. There came upon me at that moment, however, a sense of appreciation of the fact that since we had left the village of the No-vans I had been far from unhappy, nor could I attribute this to aught else than the companionship of Nah-ee-lah—a realization that convinced me that I should be utterly miserable were she to be taken from me now. Was I to submit supinely then, to capture and slavery for myself and worse than death for Nah-ee-lah, with the assurance of consequent separation from her? No. I held up my hand as a signal for the advancing Kalkars to halt.

"Stop!" I commanded. "Before you advance farther I wish to know your intentions toward us. We entered this tunnel, mistaking it for that which led to the city of my companion. Permit us to depart in peace and all will be well."

"All will be well, anyway," replied the leader of the Kalkars. "You are a strange creature, such as I have never before seen in Va-nah. Of you we know nothing except that you are not of the Kalkars, and therefore an enemy of the Kalkars, but this other is from Laythe."

"You will not permit us to go in peace, then?" I demanded.

He laughed sneeringly. "Nor in any other way," he said.

The Moon Maid

I had been standing in the aisle, with my hand upon one of the chairs near the rostrum and now I turned to Nah-ee-lah who was standing close beside me.

"Come," I said to her, "follow me; stay close behind me."

Several of the Kalkars were coming down the main aisle toward us, and as I turned toward them from speaking to Nah-ee-lah, I raised the chair which my hand had been resting upon, and swinging it quickly around my head hurled it full in the face of the leader. As he went down Nah-ee-lah and I ran forward, gaining a little toward the opening of the tunnel, and then without pausing I hurled another chair and a third and a fourth, in rapid succession. The Kalkars tried to bring us down with their lances, but they were so busy dodging chairs that they could not cast their weapons accurately, and even those few which might otherwise have struck us were warded off by my rather remarkable engines of defense.

There had been four Kalkars advancing toward us down the center aisle. The balance of the party had divided, half of it circling the cave to the left and the other half to the right, with the evident intention of coming up the center aisle from behind us. This maneuver had started just before I commenced hurling chairs at the four directly in front of us, and now when those who had intended to take us from the rear discovered that we were likely to make our way through to the tunnel's entrance, some of them sprang toward us along the passageways between the chairs, which necessitated my turning and devoting a moment's attention to them. One huge fellow was in the lead, coming across the backs of the chairs leaping from seat to seat; and being the closest to me, he was naturally my first target. The chairs were rather heavy and the one that I let drive at him caught him full in the chest with an impact that brought a howl from him and toppled him over across the backs of the chairs behind him, where he hung limp and motionless. Then I turned my attention again to those before us, all of whom had fallen before my massive ammunition. Three of them lay still, but one of them had scrambled to his feet and was in the very act of casting his lance as I looked. I stopped the weapon with a chair and as the fellow went down I caught a glimpse of Nah-ee-lah from the corners of my eyes as she snatched the lance from the first Kalkar who had fallen and hurled it at someone behind me. I heard a scream of rage and pain and then I turned in time to see another of the Kalkars fall almost at my feet, the lance imbedded in his heart.

The way before us was temporarily open, while the Kalkars behind us had paused, momentarily, at least, in evident consternation at the havoc I wrought with these

88

unseemly weapons against which they had no defense.

"Get two knives and two lances from those who have fallen," I cried to Nah-ee-lah, "while I hold these others back."

She did as I bade, and slowly we backed toward the mouth of the tunnel. My chairs had accounted for half our enemies when at last we stood in the opening, each armed with a lance and a knife.

"Now run, Nah-ee-lah, as you never ran before," I whispered to my companion. "I can hold them off until you have reached the mouth of the tunnel and clambered to the rim of the crater. If I am lucky, I will follow you."

"I will not leave you, Julian," she replied, "we will go together or not at all."

"But you must, Nah-ee-lah," I insisted, "it is for you that I have been fighting them. What difference can it make in my fate where I am when in Va-nah—all here are my enemies."

She laid her hand gently upon my arm. "I will not leave you, Julian," she repeated, "and that is final."

The Kalkars within the room were now advancing toward us menacingly.

"Halt!" I cried to them, "you see what fate your companions have met, because you would not let us go in peace. That is all we ask. I am armed now and it will be death to any who follow us."

They paused and I saw them whispering together as Nah-ee-lah and I backed along the corridor, a turn in which soon shut them from our view. Then we wheeled and ran like deer along the winding passageway. I did not feel very safe from capture at any time, but at least I breathed a sigh of relief after we had passed the chamber from which the Kalkars had run us into the cul-de-sac, and we had seen no sign of any other of their kind. We heard no sound of pursuit, but that in itself meant nothing, since the Kalkars are shod with soft leather sandals, the material for which, like all their other leather trappings, is made of the skins of Va-gas and of the prisoners from Laythe.

As we came to the pile of hooked poles which marked the last turn before the entrance of the tunnel I breathed an inward sigh of relief. Stooping, I gathered them all in my arms, and then we ran on to the opening into the crater, where I cast all but one of the poles into the abyss. That which I retained I hooked over the lip of the crater and then, turning to Nah-ee-lah, I bade her ascend.

"You should have saved two of the poles," she said, "and then we could have ascended together; but I will make haste and you can follow me immediately, for we do not know but that they are pursuing us. I cannot imagine that they will let us escape thus easily."

Even as she spoke I heard the soft patter of sandal shod feet up the corridor.

"Make haste, Nah-ee-lah," I cried; "they come!"

Climbing a pole is slow work at best, but when one is suspended over the brink of a bottomless chasm and is none too sure of the security of the hook that is holding the pole above, one must needs move cautiously. Yet, even so, Nah-ee-lah scrambled upward so rapidly as to fill me with apprehension for her safety. Nor were my fears entirely groundless, for standing in the mouth of the tunnel, where I could keep one eye upon Nah-ee-lah and the other toward the turn around which my pursuers would presently come in view, I saw the girl's hands grasp the rim of the crater at the very instant that the hook came loose and the pole dropped past me into the abyss. I might have caught it as it fell, but my whole mind was fixed upon Nah-ee-lah and her grave danger. Would she be able to draw herself upward, or would she fall? I saw her straining frantically to raise her body above the edge of the volcano, and then from up the corridor behind me came an exultant cry and I turned to face a brawny Kalkar who was racing toward me.

The City of Kalkars

NOW, indeed, did I have reason to curse the stupidity that had permitted me to cast into the abyss all of the hooked poles save one, since even this one was now lost to me and I was utterly without means of escape from the tunnel.

As the fellow approached me at a rapid run I hurled my lance, but being unaccustomed to the weapon, I missed, and then he was upon me, dropping his own lance as he leaped for me, for it was evidently his desire to take me alive and unharmed. I thought that I was going to have him now, for I believed that I was more than a match for him, but there are tricks in every method of attack and this lunar warrior was evidently well schooled in his own methods of offense. He scarcely seemed to touch me, and yet he managed to trip me and push me simultaneously so that I fell heavily backward to the ground and turning a little sideways as I fell, I must have struck my head against the side of the tunnel, for that is the last that I remember until I regained consciousness in the very cave that Nah-ee-lah and I had reached when we saw the first of the Kalkars. I was surrounded by a party of eight of the Kalkars, two of whom were half carrying, half dragging me. I learned later that in the fight before the rostrum I had killed four of their number.

The fellow who had captured me was in very good humor, doubtless because of his success, and when he discovered that I had regained consciousness he started to converse with me.

"You thought that you could escape from Gapth, did you?" he cried, "but never; you might escape from the others, but not from me—no, not from Gapth."

"I did the principal thing that I desired to do," I replied, wishing to learn if Nah-ee-lah had escaped.

"What is that?" demanded Gapth.

"I succeeded in accomplishing the escape of my companion," I replied.

He made a wry face at that. "If Gapth had been there a moment earlier she would not have escaped, either," he said, and by that I knew that she had escaped, unless she had fallen back into the crater; and I was amply repaid for my own capture if it had won freedom for Nah-ee-lah.

"Although I did not escape this time," I said, "I shall next time."

He laughed a nasty laugh. "There will be no next time," he said, "for we are taking you to the city, and once there, there is no escape, for this is the only avenue by which you can reach the outer world and once within the city you never can retrace your steps to the mouth of the tunnel."

I was not so sure of that, myself, for my sense of direction and that of location are very well developed within me. The degree of perfection attained in orientation by many officers of the International Peace Fleet has been described as almost miraculous, and even among such as these my ability in this line was a matter of comment. I was glad, therefore, that the fellow had warned me, since now I should be particularly upon the watch for each slightest scrap of information that would fix in my memory whatever route I might be led over. From the cave in which I regained consciousness there was but a single route to the mouth of the tunnel, but from here on into the city I must watch every turn and fork and crossing and draw upon the tablets of my memory an accurate and detailed map of the entire route.

"We do not even have to confine our prisoners," continued Gapth, "after we have so marked them that their ownership may always be determined."

"How do you mark them?" I asked.

"With heated irons we make the mark of the owner here," and he touched my forehead just above my eyes.

The Moon Maid

"Pleasant," I thought to myself, and then aloud: "Shall I belong to you?"

"I do not know," he replied, "but you will belong to whomever The Twenty-four allot you."

We moved on after we left the cave for a considerable period of time in silence. I was busy making mental notes of every salient feature that might be useful to me in retracing my steps, but I found nothing other than a winding and gently ascending corridor, without crossings or branches, until we reached the foot of a long flight of stone steps at the summit of which we emerged into a large chamber in the walls of which there must have been at least a dozen doorways, where, to my great disappointment, I was immediately blind-folded. They whirled me around then, but evidently it was done perfunctorily, since it was exactly one full turn and I was halted in my tracks facing precisely in the same direction that I had been before. This I was positive of, for our powers of orientation are often tested in this way in the air service. Then they marched me straight forward across the room through a doorway directly opposite that at which I had entered the chamber. I could tell when we left the larger chamber and entered the corridor from the different sound which our footsteps made. We advanced along this corridor ninety-seven paces, when we turned abruptly to the right and at the end of thirty-three paces emerged into another chamber, as I could easily tell again from the sound of our footsteps the instant we crossed the threshold. They led me about this chamber a couple of times with the evident intention of bewildering me, but in this they did not succeed, for when they turned again into a corridor I knew that it was the same corridor from which I had just emerged and that I was retracing my steps. This time they took me back thirty-three paces and then turned abruptly to the right. I could not but smile to myself when I realized that we were now continuing directly along the same corridor as that which we had entered immediately after they had first blindfolded me, their little excursion through the short corridor into the second chamber having been but a ruse to bewilder me. A moment later, at the foot of a flight of steps they removed the blind, evidently satisfied that there was now no chance of my being able to retrace my steps and find the main tunnel leading to the crater, while, as a matter of fact, I could easily have retraced every foot of it blindfolded.

From here on we climbed interminable stairways, passed through numerous corridors and chambers, all of which were illuminated by the radium-bearing substance which coated their walls and ceilings, and then we emerged suddenly upon a terrace into the open air, and I obtained my first view of a lunar city. It was built around a crater, and the buildings were terraced back from the rim, the terraces being generally devoted to the raising of garden truck and the principal fruit-bearing trees and shrubs. The city extended upward several hundred feet, the houses, as I learned later, being built one upon another, the great majority of them, therefore, being without windows looking upon the outer world.

I was led along the terrace for a short distance, and during this brief opportunity for observation I deduced that the cultivated terraces lay upon the roofs of the tier of buildings next below. To my right I could see the terraced steps extending downward to the rim of the crater. Nearly all the terraces were covered with vegetation, and in numerous places I saw what appeared to be Va-gas feeding upon the plants, and this I later learned was the fact, and that the Kalkars, when they are able to capture members of the race of Va-gas, keep them in captivity and breed them as we breed cattle, for their flesh. It is necessary, to some extent, to change the diet of the Va-gas almost exclusively to vegetation, though this diet is supplemented by the flesh of the Kalkars, and their Laythean slaves who die, the Va-gas thus being compelled to serve the double purpose of producing flesh for the Kalkars and acting as their scavengers as well.

Upon my left were the faces of buildings, uniformly two stories in height, with an occasional slender tower rising fifteen, twenty or sometimes as high as thirty feet from the terraced roofs above. It was into one of these buildings that my captors led me after we had proceeded a short distance along the terrace, and I found myself in a large apartment in which were a number of male Kalkars, and at a desk facing the entrance a large, entirely bald man who appeared to be of considerable age. To this person I was led by Gapth, who narrated my capture and the escape of Na-ee-lah.

The fellow before whom I had been brought questioned me briefly. He made no comment when I told him that I was from another world, but he examined my garments rather carefully and then after a moment turned to Gapth.

"We will hold him for questioning by The Twenty-four," he said. "If he is not of Va-nah he is neither Kalkar nor Laythean, and consequently, he must be flesh of a lower order and therefore may be eaten." He paused a moment and fell to examining a large book which seemed to be filled with plans upon which strange hieroglyphics appeared. He turned over several leaves, and finally coming evidently to the page he sought, he ran a forefinger slowly over it until it came to rest near the center of the page. "You may confine him here," he said to Gapth, "in chamber eight of the twenty-fourth section, at the seventh elevation, and you will produce him upon orders from The Twenty-four when next they meet," and then to me: "It is impossible for you to escape from the city, but if you attempt it, it may be difficult for us to find you again immediately and when we do you will be tortured to death as an example to other slaves. Go!"

I went; following Gapth and the others who had conducted me to the presence of this creature. They led me back into the very corridor from which we had emerged upon the terrace and then straight into the heart of that amazing pile for fully half a mile, where they shoved me roughly into an apartment at the right of the corridor with the admonition that I stay there until I was wanted.

I found myself in a dimly lighted, rectangular room, the air of which was very poor, and at the first glance I discovered that I was not alone, for upon a bench against the opposite wall sat a man. He looked up as I entered and I saw that his features were very fine and that he had black hair like Nah-ee-lah. He looked at me for a moment with a puzzled expression in his eyes and then he addressed me.

"You, too, are a slave?" he asked.

"I am not a slave," I replied, "I am a prisoner."

"It is all the same," he said; "but from whence come you? I have never seen your like before in Va-nah."

"I do not come from Va-nah," I replied, and then I briefly explained my origin and how I came to be in his world. He did not understand me, I am sure, for although he seemed to be, and really was, highly intelligent, he could not conceive of any condition concerning which he had had no experience and in this way he did not differ materially from intelligent and highly educated Earth Men.

"And you," I asked, at length—"you are not a Kalkar? From whence come you?"

"I am from Laythe," he replied. "I fell outside the city and was captured by one of their hunting parties."

"Why all this enmity," I asked, "between the men of Laythe and the Kalkars —who are the Kalkars, anyway?"

"You are not of Va-nah," he said, "that I can see, or you would not ask these questions. The Kalkars derive their name from a corruption of a word meaning The Thinkers. Ages ago we were one race, a prosperous people living at peace with all the world of Va-nah. The Va-gas we bred for flesh, as we do today within our own city of Laythe and as the Kalkars do within their city. Our cities, towns and villages

94

covered the slopes of the mountains and stretched downward to the sea. No corner of the three oceans but knew our ships, and our cities were joined together by a network of routes along which passed electrically driven trains"—he did not use the word trains, but an expression which might be liberally translated as ships of the land —"while other great carriers flew through the air. Our means of communication between distant points were simplified by science through the use of electrical energy, with the result that those who lived in one part of Va-nah could talk with those who lived in any other part of Va-nah, though it were to the remotest ends of the world. There were ten great divisions, each ruled by its Jemadar, and each division vied with all the others in the service which it rendered to its people. There were those who held high positions and those who held low; there were those who were rich and those who were poor, but the favors of the state were distributed equally among them, and the children of the poor had the same opportunities for education as the children of the rich, and there it was that our troubles first started. There is a saying among us that 'no learning is better than a little,' and I can well believe this true when I consider the history of my world, where, as the masses became a little educated, there developed among them a small coterie that commenced to find fault with everyone who had achieved greater learning or greater power than they. Finally, they organized themselves into a secret society called The Thinkers, but known more accurately to the rest of Va-nah as those who thought that they thought. It is a long story, for it covers a great period of time, but the result was that, slowly at first, and later rapidly, The Thinkers, who did more talking than thinking, filled the people with dissatisfaction, until at last they arose and took over the government and commerce of the entire world. The Jemadars were overthrown and the ruling class driven from power, the majority of them being murdered, though some managed to escape, and it was these, my ancestors, who founded the city of Laythe. It is believed that there are other similar cities in remote parts of Va-nah inhabited by the descendants of the Jemadar and noble classes, but Laythe is the only one of which we have knowledge. The Thinkers would not work, and the result was that both government and commerce fell into rapid decay. They not only had neither the training nor the intelligence to develop new things, but they could not carry out the old that had been developed for them. The arts and sciences languished and died with commerce and government, and Va-nah fell back into barbarism. The Va-gas saw their chance and threw off the yoke that had held them through countless ages. As the Kalkars had driven the noble class into the lofty mountains, so the Va-gas drove the Kalkars. Practically every vestige of the ancient culture and commercial advancement of Va-nah has been wiped from the face of the world. The Laytheans have held their own for many centuries, but their numbers have not increased.

"Many generations elapsed before the Laytheans found sanctuary in the city of Laythe, and during that period they, too, lost all touch with the science and advancement and the culture of the past. Nor was there any way in which to rebuild what the Kalkars had torn down, since they had destroyed every written record and every book in every library in Va-nah. And so occupied are both races in eking out a precarious existence that there is little likelihood that there will ever again be any advancement made along these lines—it is beyond the intellectual powers of the Kalkars, and the Laytheans are too weak numerically to accomplish aught."

"It does look hopeless," I said, "almost as hopeless as our situation. There is no escape, I imagine, from this Kalkar city, is there?"

"No," he said, "none whatever. There is only one avenue and we are so confused when we are brought into the city that it would be impossible for us to find our way out again through this labyrinth of corridors and chambers."

"And if we did win our way to the outer world we would be as bad off, I presume, for we could never find Laythe, and sooner or later would be recaptured by the Kalkars or taken by the Va-gas. Am I not right?"

"No," he said, "you are not right. If I could reach the rim of the crater beyond this city I could find my way to Laythe. I know the way well, for I am one of Ko-tah's hunters and am thoroughly familiar with the country for great distances in all directions from Laythe."

So this was one of Ko-tah's men. I was glad, indeed, that I had not mentioned Nah-ee-lah or told him of her possible escape, or of my acquaintance with her.

"And who is Ko-tah?" I asked, feigning ignorance.

"Ko-tah is the most powerful noble of Laythe," he replied, "some day he will be Jemadar, for now that Nah-ee-lah, the Princess, is dead, and Sagroth, the Jemadar, grows old, it will not be long before there is a change."

"And if the Princess should return to Laythe," I asked, "would Ko-tah still become Jemadar then, upon the death of Sagroth?"

"He would become Jemadar in any event," replied my companion, "for had the Princess not been carried off by the air that runs away, Ko-tah would have married her, unless she refused, in which event she might have died— people do die, you know."

"You feel no loyalty, then," I asked, "for your old Jemadar, Sagroth, or for his daughter, the Princess?"

"On the contrary, I feel every loyalty toward them, but like many others, I am afraid of Ko-tah, for he is very powerful and we know that sooner or later he will become ruler of Laythe. That is why so many of the high nobles have attached themselves to him—it is not through love of Ko-tah, but through fear that he recruits his ranks."

"But the Princess!" I exclaimed, "would the nobles not rally to her defense?"

"What would be the use?" he asked. "We of Laythe do but exist in the narrow confines of our prison city. There is no great future to which we may look forward in this life, but future incarnations may hold for us a brighter prospect. It is no cruelty, then, to kill those who exist now under the chaotic reign of anarchy which has reduced Va-nah to a wilderness."

I partially caught his rather hopeless point of view and realized that the fellow was not bad or disloyal at heart, but like all his race, reduced to a state of hopelessness that was the result of ages of retrogression to which they could see no end.

"I can find the way to the mouth of the tunnel where it opens into the crater," I told him. "But how can we reach it unarmed through a city populated with our enemies who would slay us on sight?"

"There are never very many people in the chambers or corridors far removed from the outer terraces, and if we were branded upon the forehead, as accepted slaves are, and your apparel was not so noticeable, we might possibly reach the tunnel without weapons."

"Yes," I said, "my clothes are a handicap. They would immediately call attention to us; yet, it is worth risking, for I know that I can find my way back to the crater and I should rather die than remain a slave of the Kalkars."

The truth of the matter was that I was not prompted so much by abhorrence of the fate that seemed in store for me, as by a desire to learn if Nah-ee-lah had escaped. I was constantly haunted by the horrid fear that her hold upon the rim of the crater had given and that she had fallen into the abyss below. Gapth had thought that she had escaped, but I knew that she might have fallen without either of us having seen her, since the pole up which she had clambered had been fastened a little beyond the opening of the tunnel, so that, had her hold become loosened, she would not have fallen directly past the aperture. The more I thought of it, the more anxious I became to reach Laythe and institute a search for her.

While we were still discussing our chances of escape, two slaves brought us food in the shape of raw vegetables and fruit. I scanned them carefully for weapons, but they had none, a circumstance to which they may owe their lives. I could have used their garments, had they been other than slaves, but I had hit upon a bolder plan than this and must wait patiently for a favorable opportunity to put it into practice.

After eating I became sleepy and was about to stretch out upon the floor of our prison when my companion, whose name was Moh-goh, told me that there was a sleeping apartment adjoining the room in which we were, that had been set apart for us.

The doorway leading to the sleeping chamber was covered by heavy hangings, and as I parted them and stepped into the adjoining chamber, I found myself in almost total darkness, the walls and ceiling of this room not having been treated with the illuminating coating used in the corridors and apartments which they wished to maintain in a lighted condition. I later learned that all their sleeping apartments were thus naturally dark. In one corner of the room was a pile of dried vegetation which I discovered must answer the purpose of mattress and covering, should I require any. However, I was not so particular, as I had been accustomed to only the roughest of fare since I had left my luxurious stateroom aboard the Barsoom. How long I slept I do not know, but I was awakened by Moh-goh calling me. He was leaning over me, shaking me by the shoulder.

"You are wanted," he whispered. "They have come to take us before The Twenty-four."

"Tell them to go to the devil," I said, for I was very sleepy and only half awake. Of course, he did not know what devil meant, but evidently he judged from my tone that my reply was disrespectful to the Kalkars.

"Do not anger them," he said, "it will only make your fate the harder. When The Twenty-four command, all must obey."

"Who are The Twenty-four?" I demanded.

"They compose the committee that rules this Kalkar city."

I was thoroughly awakened now and rose to my feet, following him into the adjoining chamber, where I saw two Kalkar warriors standing impatiently awaiting us. As I saw them a phrase leaped to my brain and kept repeating itself: "There are but two, there are but two."

They were across the room from us, standing by the entrance, and Moh-goh was close to me.

"There are but two," I whispered to him in a low voice, "you take one and I will take the other. Do you dare?"

"I will take the one at the right," he replied, and together we advanced across the room slowly toward the unsuspecting warriors. The moment that we were in reach of them we leaped for them simultaneously. I did not see how Moh-goh attacked his man, for I was busy with my own, though it took me but an instant to settle him, for I struck him a single terrific blow upon the chin and as he fell I leaped upon him, wresting his dagger from its scabbard and plunging it into his heart before he could regain his senses from the stunning impact of my fist. Then I turned to assist Moh-goh, only to discover that he needed no assistance, but was already arising from the body of his antagonist, whose throat was cut from ear to ear with his own weapon.

"Quick!" I cried to Moh-goh, "drag them into the sleeping apartment before we are discovered," and a moment later we had deposited the two corpses in the dimly lighted apartment adjoining.

"We will leave the city as Kalkar warriors," I said, commencing to strip the accoutrements and garments from the man I had slain.

Moh-goh grinned. "Not a bad idea," he said. "If you can find the route to the crater it is possible that we may yet escape."

It took us but a few moments to effect the change, and after we had hidden the bodies beneath the vegetation that had served us as a bed and stepped out into the other chamber, where we could have a good look at one another, we realized that if we were not too closely scrutinized we might pass safely through the corridors beneath the Kalkar city, for the Kalkars are a mongrel breed, comprising many divergent types. My complexion, which differed outrageously from that of either the Kalkars or the Laytheans, constituted our greatest danger, but we must take the chance, and at least we were armed.

"Lead the way," said Moh-goh, "and if you can find the crater I can assure you that I can find Laythe."

"Very good," I said, "come," and stepping into the corridor I moved off confidently in the direction that I knew I should find the passageways and stairs along which I had been conducted from the crater tunnel. I was as confident of success as though I were traversing the most familiar precinct of my native city.

We traveled a considerable distance without meeting anyone, and at last reached the chamber in which I had been blindfolded. As we entered it I saw fully a score of Kalkars lolling upon benches or lying upon vegetation that was piled upon the floor. They looked up as we entered, and at the same time Moh-goh stepped in front of me.

"Who are you and where are you going?" demanded one of the Kalkars.

"By order of The Twenty-four," said Moh-goh, and stepped into the room. Instantly I realized that he did not know in which direction to go, and that by his hesitancy all might be lost.

"Straight ahead, straight across the room," I whispered to him, and he stepped out briskly in the direction of the entrance to the tunnel. Fortunately for us, the chamber was not brilliantly lighted, and the Kalkars were at the far end of it; otherwise they must certainly have discovered my deception, at least, since any sort of close inspection would have revealed the fact that I was not of Va-nah. However, they did not halt us, though I was sure that I saw one of them eyeing me suspiciously, and I venture to say that I took the last twenty steps without drawing a breath.

It was quickly over, however, and we had entered the tunnel which now led without further confusing ramifications directly to the crater.

"We were fortunate," I said to Moh-goh.

"That we were," he replied.

In silence, then, that we might listen for pursuit, or for the sound of Kalkars ahead of us, we hastened rapidly along the descending passageway toward the mouth of the tunnel where it opened into the crater; and at last, as we rounded the last turn and I saw the light of day ahead of me, I breathed a deep sigh of relief, though almost simultaneously my happiness turned to despair at the sudden recollection that there were no hooked poles here to assist us to the summit of the crater wall. What were we to do?

"Moh-goh," I said, turning to my companion as we halted at the end of the tunnel, "there are no poles with which to ascend. I had forgotten it, but in order to prevent the Kalkars from ascending after me, I threw all but one into the abyss, and that one slipped from the rim and was lost also, just as my pursuers were about to seize me."

I had not told Moh-goh that I had had a companion, since it would be difficult to answer any questions he might propound on the subject without revealing the identity of Nah-ee-lah.

Edgar Rice Burroughs

"Oh, we can overcome that," replied my companion. "We have these two spears, which are extremely stout, and inasmuch as we shall have plenty of time, we can easily arrange them in some way that will permit us to ascend to the summit of the crater. It is very fortunate that we were not pursued."

The Kalkar's spears had a miniature crescent-shaped hook at the base of their point similar to the larger ones affected by the Va-gas. Moh-goh thought that we could fasten the two spears securely together and then catch the small hook of the upper one upon the rim of the crater, testing its hold thoroughly before either of us attempted to ascend. Beneath his tunic he wore a rope coiled around his waist which he explained to me was a customary part of the equipment of all Laytheans. It was his idea to tie one end of this around the waist of whichever of us ascended first, the other going as far back into the tunnel as possible and bracing himself, so that in the event that the climber fell, he would be saved from death, though I figured that he would get a rather nasty shaking up and some bad bruises, under the best of circumstances.

I volunteered to go first and began fastening one end of the rope securely about my waist while Moh-goh made the two spears fast together with a short length that he had cut from the other end. He worked rapidly, with deft, nimble fingers, and seemed to know pretty well what he was doing. In the event that I reached the summit in safety, I was to pull up the spears and then haul Moh-goh up by the rope.

Having fastened the rope to my satisfaction, I stood as far out upon the ledge before the entrance to the tunnel as I safely could, and with my back toward the crater looked up at the rim twenty feet above me, in a vain attempt to select from below, if possible, a reasonably secure point upon which to hook the spear. As I stood thus upon the edge of eternity, steadying myself with one hand against the tunnel wall, there came down to me from out of the tunnel a noise which I could not mistake. Moh-goh heard it, too, and looked at me, with a rueful shake of his head and a shrug of his shoulders.

"Everything is against us, Earth Man," he said, for this was the name he had given me when I told him what my world was called.

A Meeting with Ko-tah

THE pursuers were not yet in sight, but I knew from the nearness of the sound of approaching footsteps that it would be impossible to complete the splicing of the

101

spears, to find a secure place for the hook above, and for me to scramble upward to the rim of the crater and haul Moh-goh after me before they should be upon us. Our position looked almost hopeless. I could think of no avenue of escape, and yet I tried, and as I stood there with bent head, my eyes cast upon the floor of the tunnel, they fell upon the neatly coiled rope lying at my feet, one end of which was fastened securely about my waist. Instantly there flashed into my mind a mad inspiration. I glanced up at the overhanging rim above me. Could I do it? There was a chance—the lesser gravity of the Moon placed the thing within the realm of possibility, and yet by all earthly standards it was impossible. I did not wait, I could not wait, for had I given the matter any thought I doubt that I would have had the nerve to attempt it. Behind me lay a cavern opening into the depths of space, into which I should be dashed if my mad plan failed; but, what of it? Better death than slavery. I stooped low, then, and concentrating every faculty upon absolute coordination of mind and muscles, I leaped straight upward with all the strength of my legs.

And in that instant during which my life hung in the balance, of what did I think? Of home, of Earth, of the friends of my childhood? No—of a pale and lovely face, with great, dark eyes and a perfect forehead, surmounted by a wealth of raven hair. It was the image of Nah-ee-lah, the Moon Maid, that I would have carried with me into eternity, had I died that instant.

But, I did not die. My leap carried me above the rim of the crater, where I lunged forward and fell sprawling, my arms and upper body upon the surface of the ground. Instantly I turned about and lying upon my belly, seized the rope in both hands.

"Quick, Moh-goh!" I cried to my companion below; "make the rope fast about you, keep hold of the spears and I will drag you up!"

"Pull away," he answered me instantly, "I have no time to make the rope fast about me. They are almost upon me, pull away and be quick about it."

I did as he bade, and a moment later his hands grasped the rim of the crater and with my assistance he gained the top, dragging the spears after him. For a moment he stood there in silence looking at me with a most peculiar expression upon his face; then he shook his head.

"I do not understand, yet," he said, "how you did it, but it was very wonderful."

"I scarcely expected to accomplish it in safety, myself," I replied, "but anything is better than slavery."

From below us came the voices of the Kalkars in angry altercation. Moh-goh picked up a fragment of rock, and leaning over the edge of the crater, threw it down among them. "I got one," he said, turning to me with a laugh, "he tumbled off into nothing; they hate that. They believe that there is no reincarnation for those who fall into a crater."

"Do you think that they will try to follow us?" I asked.

"No," he said, "they will be afraid to use their hooked poles here for a long time, lest we should be in the neighborhood and shove them off into the crater. I will drop another rock down if any of them are in sight and then we will go upon our way. I do not fear them here in the hills, anyway. There is always plenty of broken stone upon the level places, and we of Laythe are trained to use it most effectively—almost as far as I can throw, I can score a hit."

The Kalkars had withdrawn into the tunnel, so Moh-goh lost his opportunity to despatch another, and presently turned away from the crater and set out into the mountains following close behind.

I can assure you that I felt much better, now that I was armed with a spear and a knife, and as we walked I practiced casting stones, at Moh-goh's suggestion and under his instruction, until I became rather proficient in the art.

I shall not weary you with a narration of our journey to Laythe. How long it took, I do not know. It may have consumed a day, a week, a month, for time seemed quite a meaningless term in Va-nah, but at length, after clambering laboriously from the bottom of a deep gorge, we stood upon the edge of a rolling plateau, and at some little distance beheld what at first appeared to be a cone-shaped mountain, rising fully a mile into the air above the surface of the plateau.

"There," cried Moh-goh, "is Laythe! The crater where lies the entrance to the tunnel leading to the city is beyond it."

As we approached the city, the base of which we must skirt in order to reach the crater beyond, I was able to obtain a better idea of the dimensions and methods of construction of this great interior lunar city, the base of which was roughly circular and about six miles in diameter, ranging from a few hundred to a thousand feet above the level of the plateau. The base of the city appeared to be the outer wall of an ancient extinct volcano, the entire summit of which had been blown off during some terrific eruption of a bygone age. Upon this base the ancient Laytheans had commenced the construction of their city, the houses of which rose one upon another as did those of the Kalkar city from which we had just escaped. The great age of Laythe was attested by the tremendous height to which these superimposed buildings had arisen, the loftiest wall of Laythe now rising fully a mile above the floor of the plateau. Narrow terraces encircled the periphery of the towering city, and as we approached more closely I saw doors and windows opening upon the terraces and figures moving to and fro, the whole resembling closely an enormous hive of bees. When we had reached a point near the base of the city, I saw that we had been discovered, for directly above us there were people at various points who were unquestionably looking down at us and commenting upon us.

"They have seen us from above," I said to Moh-goh, "why don't you hail them?"

"They take us for Kalkars," he replied. "It is easier for us to enter the city by way of the tunnel, where I shall have no difficulty in establishing my identity."

"If they think we are Kalkars," I said, "will they not attack us?"

"No," he replied, "Kalkars often pass Laythe. If they do not try to enter the city, we do not molest them."

"Your people fear them, then?" I asked.

"It practically amounts to that," he replied. "They greatly outnumber us, perhaps a thousand to one, and as they are without justice, mercy or honor we try not to antagonize them unnecessarily."

We came at length to the mouth of the crater, and here Moh-goh looped his rope about the base of a small tree growing close to the rim and slipped down to the opening of the tunnel directly beneath. I followed his example, and when I was beside him Moh-goh pulled the rope in, coiled it about his waist, and we set off along the passageway leading toward Laythe.

After my long series of adventures with unfriendly people in Va-nah, I had somewhat the sensation of one returning home after a long absence, for Moh-goh had assured me that the people of Laythe would receive me well and that I should be treated as a friend. He even assured me that he would procure for me a good berth in the service of Ko-tah. My greatest regret now was for Nah-ee-lah, and that she was not my companion, instead of Moh-goh. I was quite sure that she was lost, for had she escaped, falling back into the crater outside the Kalkar city, I doubted that she could successfully have found her way to Laythe. My heart had been heavy since we had been separated, and I had come to realize that the friendship of this little Moon Maid had meant a great deal more to me than I had thought. I could scarcely think of her now without a lump coming into my throat, for it seemed cruel, indeed, that one so young and lovely should have met so untimely an end.

The distance between the crater and the city of Laythe is not great, and presently we came directly out upon the lower terrace within the city. This terrace is at the very rim of the crater around which Laythe is built. And here we ran directly into the arms of a force of about fifty warriors.

Moh-goh emerged from the tunnel with his spear grasped in both hands high above his head, the point toward the rear, and I likewise, since he had cautioned me to do so. So surprised were the warriors to see any creatures emerge from this tunnel, which had been so long disused, that we were likely to have been slain before they realized that we had come before them with the signal of peace.

The guard that is maintained at the inner opening of the tunnel is considered by the Laytheans as more or less of an honorary assignment, the duties of which are performed perfunctorily.

"What do you here, Kalkars?" exclaimed the commander of the guard.

"We are not Kalkars," replied my companion. "I am Moh-goh the Paladar, and this be my friend. Can it be that you, Ko-vo the Kamadar, do not know me?"

"Ah!" cried the commander of the guard, "it is, indeed, Moh-goh the Paladar. You have been given up as lost."

"I was lost, indeed, had it not been for this, my friend," replied Moh-goh, nodding his head in my direction. "I was captured by the Kalkars and incarcerated in City No. 337."

"You escaped from a Kalkar city?" exclaimed Ko-vo, in evident incredulity. "That is impossible. It never has been accomplished."

"But we did accomplish it," replied Moh-goh, "thanks to my friend here," and then he narrated briefly to Ko-vo the details of our escape.

"It scarce seems possible," commented the Laythean, when Moh-goh had completed his narrative, "and what may be the name of your friend, Moh-goh, and from what country did you say he came?"

"He calls himself Ju-lan-fit," replied Moh-goh, for that was as near as he could come to the pronunciation of my name. And so it was that as Ju-lan-fit I was known to the Laytheans as long as I remained among them. They thought that fifth, which they pronounced "fit," was a title similar to one of those which always followed the name of its possessor in Laythe, as Sagroth the Jemadar, or Emperor; Ko-vo the Kamadar, a title which corresponds closely to that of the English Duke; and Moh-goh the Paladar, or Count. And so, to humor them, I told them that it meant the same as their Javadar, or Prince. I was thereafter called sometimes Ju-lan-fit, and sometimes Ju-lan Javadar, as the spirit moved him who addressed me.

At Moh-goh's suggestion, Ko-vo the Kamadar detailed a number of his men to accompany us to Moh-goh's dwelling, lest we have difficulty in passing through the city in our Kalkar garb.

As we had stood talking with Ko-vo, my eyes had been taking in the interior sights of this lunar city. The crater about which Laythe is built appeared to be between three and four miles in width, the buildings facing it and rising terrace upon terrace to a height of a mile at least, were much more elaborate of architecture and far richer in carving than those of the Kalkar City No. 337. The terraces were broad and well cultivated, and as we ascended toward Moh-goh's dwelling I saw that much pains had been taken to elaborately landscape many of them, there being pools and rivulets and waterfalls in numerous places. As in the Kalkar city, there were Va-gas fattening for food in little groups upon various terraces. They were sleek and fat and appeared contented, and I learned later that they were perfectly satisfied with their lot, having no more conception of the purpose for which they were bred or the fate that awaited them than have the beef cattle of Earth.

The U-gas of Laythe have induced this mental state in their Va-gas herds by a process of careful selection covering a period of ages, possibly, during which time they have conscientiously selected for breeding purposes the most stupid and unimaginative members of their herds.

At Moh-goh's dwelling we were warmly greeted by the members of his family —his father, mother and two sisters—all of whom, like the other Laytheans I had seen, were of striking appearance. The men were straight and handsome, the women physically perfect and of great beauty.

I could see in the affectionate greetings which they exchanged an indication of a family life and ties similar to those which are most common upon Earth, while their gracious and hospitable reception of me marked them as people of highly refined sensibilities. First of all they must hear Moh-goh's story, and then, after having congratulated us and praised us, they set about preparing baths and fresh apparel for us, in which they were assisted by a corps of servants, descendants, I was told, of the faithful servitors who had remained loyal to the noble classes and accompanied them in their exile.

We rested for a short time after our baths, and then Moh-goh announced that he must go before Ko-tah, to whom it was necessary that he report, and that he would take me with him. I was appareled now in raiment befitting my supposed rank and carried the weapons of a Laythean gentleman—a short lance, or javelin, a dagger and a sword, but with my relatively darker skin and my blond hair, I could never hope to be aught than an object of remark in any Laythean company. Owing to the color of my hair, some of them thought that I was a Kalkar, but upon this score my complexion set them right.

Ko-tah's dwelling was, indeed, princely, stretching along a broad terrace for fully a quarter of a mile, with its two stories and its numerous towers and minarets. The entire face of the building was elaborately and beautifully carved, the decorations in their entirety recording pictographically the salient features of the lives of Ko-tah's ancestors.

Armed nobles stood on either side of the massive entrance way, and long before we reached this lunar prince I realized that possibly he was more difficult to approach than one of earthly origin, but at last we were ushered into his presence, and Moh-goh, with the utmost deference, presented me to Ko-tah the Javadar. Having assumed a princely title and princely raiment, I chose to assume princely prerogatives as well, believing that my position among the Laytheans would be better assured and all my interests furthered if they thought me of royal blood, and so I acknowledged my introduction to Ko-tah as though we were equals and that he was being presented to me upon the same footing that I was being presented to him.

I found him, like all his fellows, a handsome man, but with a slightly sinister expression which I did not like. Possibly I was prejudiced against him from what Nah-ee-lah had told me, but be that as it may, I conceived a dislike and distrust for him the moment that I laid eyes upon him, and I think, too, that he must have sensed my attitude, for, though he was outwardly gracious and courteous, I believe that Ko-tah the Javadar never liked me.

It is true that he insisted upon allotting me quarters within his palace and that he gave me service high among his followers, but I was at that time a novelty among them, and Ko-tah was not alone among the royalty who would have been glad to have entertained me and showered favors upon me, precisely as do Earth Men when a titled stranger, or famous man from another land, comes to their country.

Although I did not care for him, I was not loth to accept his hospitality, since I felt that because of my friendship for Nah-ee-lah I owed all my loyalty to Sagroth the Jemadar, and if by placing myself in the camp of the enemy I might serve the father of Nah-ee-lah, I was justified in so doing.

The Moon Maid

I found myself in a rather peculiar position in the palace of Ko-tah, since I was supposed to know little or nothing of internal conditions in Laythe, and yet had learned from both Nah-ee-lah and Moh-goh a great deal concerning the intrigues and politics of this lunar city. For example, I was not supposed to know of the existence of Nah-ee-lah. Not even did Moh-goh know that I had heard of her; and so until her name was mentioned, I could ask no questions concerning her, though I was anxious indeed to discover if by any miracle of chance, she had returned in safety to Laythe, or if aught had been learned concerning her fate.

Ko-tah held me in conversation for a considerable period of time, asking many questions concerning Earth and my voyage from that planet to the Moon. I knew that he was skeptical, and yet he was a man of such intelligence as to realize that there must be something in the Universe beyond his understanding or his knowledge. His eyes told him that I was not a native of Va-nah, and his ears must have corroborated the testimony of his eyes, for try as I would, I never was able to master the Va-nahan language so that I could pass for a native.

At the close of our interview Ko-tah announced that Moh-goh would also remain in quarters in the palace, suggesting that if it was agreeable to me, my companion should share my apartments with me.

"Nothing would give me greater pleasure, Ko-tah the Javadar," I said, "than to have my good friend, Moh-goh the Paladar, always with me."

"Excellent!" exclaimed Ko-tah. "You must both be fatigued. Go, therefore, to your apartments and rest. Presently I will repair to the palace of the Jemadar with my court, and you will be notified in sufficient time to prepare yourselves to accompany me."

The audience was at an end, and we were led by nobles of Ko-tah's palace to our apartments, which lay upon the second floor in pleasant rooms overlooking the terraces down to the brink of the great, yawning crater below.

Until I threw myself upon the soft mattress that served as a bed for me, I had not realized how physically exhausted I had been. Scarcely had I permitted myself to relax in the luxurious ease which precedes sleep ere I was plunged into profound slumber, which must have endured for a considerable time, since when I awoke I was completely refreshed. Moh-goh was already up and in the bath, a marble affair fed by a continuous supply of icy water which originated among the ice-clad peaks of the higher mountains behind Laythe. The bather had no soap, but used rough fibre gloves with which he rubbed the surface of his skin until it glowed. These baths rather took one's breath away, but amply repaid for the shock by the sensation of exhilaration and well being which resulted from them.

In addition to private baths in each dwelling, each terrace supported a public bath, in which men, women and children disported themselves, recalling to my mind the ancient Roman baths which earthly history records.

The baths of the Jemadar which I was later to see in the palace of Sagroth were marvels of beauty and luxury. Here, when the Emperor entertains, his guests amuse themselves by swimming and diving, which, from what I have been able to judge, are the national sports of the Laytheans. The Kalkars care less for the water, while the Va-gas only enter it through necessity.

I followed Moh-goh in the bath, in which my first sensation was that I was freezing to death. While we were dressing a messenger from Ko-tah summoned us to his presence, with instructions that we were to be prepared to accompany him to the palace of Sagroth the Jemadar.

Growing Danger

THE palace of the Emperor stands, a magnificent pile, upon the loftiest terrace of Laythe, extending completely around the enormous crater. There are but three avenues leading to it from the terraces below—three magnificent stairways, each of which may be closed by enormous gates of stone, apparently wrought from huge slabs and intricately chiselled into marvelous designs, so that at a distance they present the appearance of magnificent lacework. Each gate is guarded by a company of fifty warriors, their tunics bearing the imperial design in a large circle over the left breast.

The ceremony of our entrance to the imperial terrace was most gorgeous and impressive. Huge drums and trumpets blared forth a challenge as we reached the foot of the stairway which we were to ascend to the palace. High dignitaries in gorgeous trappings came down the steps to meet us, as if to formally examine the credentials of Ko-tah and give official sanction to his entrance. We were then conducted through the gateway across a broad terrace beautifully landscaped and ornamented by statuary that was most evidently the work of finished artists. These works of art comprised both life size and heroic figures of individuals and groups, and represented for the most part historic or legendary figures and events of the remote past, though there were also likenesses of all the rulers of Laythe, up to and including Sagroth the present Jemadar.

Upon entering the palace we were led to a banquet hall, where we were served with food, evidently purely in accordance with ancient court ceremonial, since there was little to eat and the guests barely tasted of that which was presented to them. This ceremony consumed but a few minutes of Earth time, following which we were conducted through spacious hallways to the throne room of the Jemadar, an apartment of great beauty and considerable size. Its decorations and lines were simple, almost to severity, yet suggesting regal dignity and magnificence. Upon a dais at the far end of the room were three thrones, that in the center being occupied by a man whom I knew at once to be Sagroth, while upon either side sat a woman.

Ko-tah advanced and made his obeisance before his ruler, and after the exchange of a few words between them Ko-tah returned and conducted me to the foot of Sagroth's throne.

I had been instructed that it was in accordance with court etiquette that I keep my eyes upon the ground until I had been presented and Sagroth had spoken to me, and that then I should be introduced to the Jemadav, or Empress, when I might raise my eyes to her, also, and afterward to the occupant of the third throne when I should be formally presented to her.

Sagroth spoke most graciously to me, and as I raised my eyes I saw before me a man of great size and evident strength of character. He was by far the most regal appearing individual my eyes had ever rested upon, while his low, well modulated, yet powerful voice accentuated the majesty of his mien. It was he who presented me to his Jemadav, whom I discovered to be a creature fully as regal in appearance as her imperial mate, and although doubtless well past middle age, still possessing remarkable beauty, in which was to be plainly noted Nah-ee-lah's resemblance to her mother.

Again I lowered my eyes as Sagroth presented me to the occupant of the third throne.

"Ju-lan the Javadar," he repeated the formal words of the presentation, "raise your eyes to the daughter of Laythe, Nah-ee-lah the Nonovar."

As my eyes, filled doubtless with surprise and incredulity, shot to the face of Nah-ee-lah, I was almost upon the verge of an exclamation of the joy and happiness which I felt in seeing her again and in knowing that she was safely returned to her parents and her city once more. But as my eyes met hers the exuberance of my spirit was as effectually and quickly checked by her cold glance and haughty mien as if I had received a blow in the face.

There was no hint of recognition in Nah-ee-lah's expression. She nodded coldly in acknowledgment of the presentation and then let her eyes pass above my head toward the opposite end of the throne room. My pride was hurt, and I was angry, but I would not let her see how badly I was hurt. I have always prided myself upon my control, and so I know that then I hid my emotion and turned once more to Sagroth, as though I had received from his daughter the Nonovar precisely the favor that I had a right to expect. If the Jemadar had noticed aught peculiar in either Nah-ee-lah's manner or mine, he gave no hint of it. He spoke again graciously to me and then dismissed me, with the remark that we should meet again later.

Having withdrawn from the throne room, Ko-tah informed me that following the audience I should have an opportunity to meet Sagroth less formally, since he had commanded that I remain in the palace as his guest during the meal which followed.

"It is a mark of distinction," said Ko-tah, "but remember, Ju-lan the Javadar, that you have accepted the friendship of Ko-tah and are his ally."

"Do not embroil me in the political intrigues of Laythe," I replied. "I am a stranger, with no interest in the internal affairs of your country, for the reason that I have no knowledge of them."

"One is either a friend or an enemy," replied Ko-tah.

"I am not sufficiently well acquainted to be accounted either," I told him; "nor shall I choose my friends in Laythe until I am better acquainted, nor shall another choose them for me."

"You are a stranger here," said Ko-tah. "I speak in your best interests, only. If you would succeed here; aye, if you would live, even, you must choose quickly and you must choose correctly. I, Ko-tah the Javadar, have spoken."

"I choose my own friends," I replied, "according to the dictates of my honor and my heart. I, Ju-lan the Javadar, have spoken."

He bowed low in acquiescence, and when he again raised his eyes to mine I was almost positive from the expression in them that his consideration of me was marked more by respect than resentment.

"We shall see," was all that he said, and withdrew, leaving me to the kindly attention of some of the gentlemen of Sagroth's court who had been standing at a respectful distance out of earshot of Ko-tah and myself. These men chatted pleasantly with me for some time until I was bidden to join Sagroth in another part of the palace.

I found myself now with a man who had evidently thrown off the restraint of a formal audience, though without in the slightest degree relinquishing either his dignity or his majesty. He spoke more freely and his manner was more democratic. He asked me to be seated, nor would he himself sit until I had, a point of Laythean court etiquette which made a vast impression on me, since it indicated that the first gentleman of the city must also be the first in courtesy. He put question after question to me concerning my own world and the means by which I had been transported to Va-nah.

"There are fragmentary, extremely fragmentary, legends handed down from extreme antiquity which suggest that our remote ancestors had some knowledge concerning the other worlds of which you speak," he said, "but these have been considered always the veriest of myths. Can it be possible that, after all, they are based upon truth?"

"The remarkable part of them," I suggested, "is that they exist at all, since it is difficult to understand how any knowledge of the outer Universe could ever reach to the buried depths of Va-nah."

"No, not by any means," he said, "if what you tell me is the truth, for our legends bear out the theory that Va-nah is located in the center of an enormous globe and that our earliest progenitors lived upon the outer surface of this globe, being forced at last by some condition which the legends do not even suggest, to find their way into this inner world."

I shook my head. It did not seem possible.

"And, yet," he said, noting the doubt that my expression evidently betrayed, "you yourself claim to have reached Va-nah from a great world far removed from our globe which you call the Moon. If you reached us from another world, is it then so difficult to believe that those who preceded us reached Va-nah from the outer crust of this Moon? It is almost an historic certainty," he continued, "that our ancestors possessed great ships which navigated the air. As you entered Va-nah by means of a similar conveyance, may not they have done likewise?"

I had to admit that it was within the range of possibilities, and in so doing, to avow that the Moon Men of antiquity had been millions of years in advance of their brethren of the Earth.

But, after all, was it such a difficult conclusion to reach when one considers the fact that the Moon being smaller, must have cooled more rapidly than Earth, and therefore, provided that it had an atmosphere, have been habitable to man ages before man could have lived upon our own planet?

We talked pleasantly upon many subjects for some time, and then, at last, Sagroth arose.

"We will join the others at the tables now," he said, and as he led the way from the apartment in which we had been conversing alone, stone doors opened before us as by magic, indicating that the Jemadar of Laythe was not only well served, but well protected, or possibly well spied upon.

After we emerged from the private audience, guards accompanied us, some preceding the Jemadar and some following, and thus we moved in semi-state through several corridors and apartments until we came out upon a balcony upon the second floor of the palace overlooking the terraces and the crater.

Here, along the rail of the balcony, were numerous small tables, each seating two, all but two of the tables being occupied by royal and noble retainers and their women. As the Jemadar entered, these all arose, facing him respectfully, and simultaneously through another entrance, came the Jemadav and Nah-ee-lah.

They stood just within the room, waiting until Sagroth and I crossed to them. While we were doing so, Sagroth very courteously explained the procedure I was to follow.

"You will place yourself upon the Nonovar's left," he concluded, "and conduct her to her table precisely as I conduct the Jemadav."

Nah-ee-lah's head was high as I approached her and she vouchsafed me only the merest inclination of it in response to my respectful salutation. In silence we followed Sagroth and his Empress to the tables reserved for us. The balance of the company remained standing until, at a signal from Sagroth, we all took our seats. It was necessary for me to watch the others closely, as I knew nothing concerning the social customs of Laythe, but when I saw that conversation had become general I glanced at Nah-ee-lah.

"The Princess of Laythe so soon forgets her friends?" I asked.

"The Princess of Laythe never forgets her friends," she replied.

"I know nothing of your customs here," I said, "but in my world even royalty may greet their friends with cordiality and seeming pleasure."

"And here, too," she retorted.

I saw that something was amiss, that she seemed to be angry with me, but the cause I could not imagine. Perhaps she thought I had deserted her at the entrance to the tunnel leading to the Kalkar city. But no, she must have guessed the truth. What then, could be the cause of her cold aloofness, who, the last that I had seen of her, had been warm with friendship?

"I wonder," I said, trying a new tack, "if you were as surprised to see me alive as I you. I had given you up for lost, Nah-ee-lah, and I had grieved more than I can tell you. When I saw you in the audience chamber I could scarce repress myself, but when I saw that you did not wish to recognize me, I could only respect your desires."

She made no reply, but turned and looked out the window across the terraces and the crater to the opposite side of Laythe. She was ice, who had been almost fire. No longer was she little Nah-ee-lah, the companion of my hardships and dangers. No longer was she friend and confidante, but a cold and haughty Princess, who evidently looked upon me with disfavor. Her attitude outraged all the sacred tenets of friendship, and I was angered.

"Princess," I said, "if it is customary for Laytheans thus to cast aside the sacred bonds of friendship, I should do as well to be among the Va-gas or the Kalkars."

"The way to either is open," she replied haughtily. "You are not a prisoner in Laythe."

Thereafter conversation languished and expired, as far at least, as Nah-ee-lah and I were concerned, and I was more than relieved when the unpleasant function was concluded.

Two young nobles took me in charge, following the meal; as it seemed that I was to remain as a guest in the palace for a while, and as I expressed a desire to see as much of the imperial residence as I might be permitted to, they graciously conducted me upon a tour of inspection. We went out upon the outer terraces which overlooked the valleys and the mountains, and never in my life have I looked upon a landscape more majestic or inspiring. The crater of Laythe, situated upon a broad plateau entirely surrounded by lofty mountains, titanic peaks that would dwarf our Alps into insignificance and reduce the Himalayas to foothills, towered far into the distance upon the upper side, the ice-clad summits of those more distant seemed to veritably topple above us, while a thousand feet below us the pinks and lavenders of the weird lunar vegetation lay like a soft carpet upon the gently undulating surface of the plateau.

But my guides seemed less interested in the scenery than in me. They plied me with questions continually, until I was more anxious to be rid of them than aught else that I could think of. They asked me a little concerning my own world and what I thought of Laythe, and if I found the Princess Nah-ee-lah charming, and my opinion of the Emperor Sagroth. My answers must have been satisfactory, for presently they came very close to me and one of them whispered:

"You need not fear to speak in our presence. We, too, are friends and followers of Ko-tah."

"The Devil!" I thought. "They are bound to embroil me in their petty intrigues. What do I care for Sagroth or Ko-tah or"—and then my thoughts reverted to Nah-ee-lah. She had treated me cruelly. Her cold aloofness and her almost studied contempt had wounded me, yet I could not say to myself that Nah-ee-lah was nothing to me. She had been my friend and I had been hers, and I should remain her friend to my dying day. Perhaps, then, if these people were bound to draw me into their political disputes, I might turn their confidences into profit for Nah-ee-lah. I had never told them that I was a creature of Ko-tah's, for I was not, nor had I ever told Ko-tah that I was an enemy to Sagroth; in fact, I had led him to believe the very opposite. And so I gave these two an evasive answer which might have meant anything, and they chose to interpret it as meaning that I was one of them. Well, what could I do? It was not my fault if they insisted upon deceiving themselves, and Nah-ee-lah might yet need the friendship that she had scorned.

"Has Sagroth no loyal followers, then," I asked, "that you are all so sure of the success of the coup d'état that Ko-tah plans?"

"Ah, you know about it then!" cried one of them. "You are in the confidence of the Javadar."

I let them think that I was. It could do no harm, at least.

"Did he tell you when it was to happen?" asked the other.

"Perhaps, already I have said too much," I replied. "The confidences of Ko-tah are not to be lightly spread about."

"You are right," said the last speaker. "It is well to be discreet, but let us assure you, Ju-lan the Javadar, that we are equally in the confidence and favor of Ko-tah with any of those who serve him; otherwise, he would not have entrusted us with a portion of the work which must be done within the very palace of the Jemadar."

"Have you many accomplices here?" I asked.

"Many," he replied, "outside of the Jemadar's guards. They remain loyal to Sagroth. It is one of the traditions of the organization, and they will die for him, to a man and," he added with a shrug, "they shall die, never fear. When the time arrives and the signal is given, each member of the guard will be set upon by two of Ko-tah's faithful followers."

I do not know how long I remained in the City of Laythe. Time passed rapidly, and I was very happy after I returned to the dwelling of Moh-goh. I swam and dived with them and their friends in the baths upon our terrace, and also in those of Ko-tah. I learned to use the flying wings that I had first seen upon Nah-ee-lah the day that she fell exhausted into the clutches of the Va-gas, and many were the lofty and delightful excursions we took into the higher mountains of the Moon, when Moh-goh or his friends organized pleasure parties for the purpose. Constantly surrounded by people of culture and refinement, by brave men and beautiful women, my time was so filled with pleasurable activities that I made no effort to gauge it. I felt that I was to spend the balance of my life here, and I might as well get from it all the pleasure that Laythe could afford.

I did not see Nah-ee-lah during all this time, and though I still heard a great deal concerning the conspiracy against Sagroth, I presently came to attach but little importance to what I did hear, after I learned that the conspiracy had been on foot for over thirteen kelds, or approximately about ten earthly years, and seemed, according to my informers, no nearer consummation than it ever had been in the past.

Time does not trouble these people much, and I was told that it might be twenty kelds before Ko-tah took action, though on the other hand, he might strike within the next ola.

There was an occurrence during this period which aroused my curiosity, but concerning which Moh-goh was extremely reticent. Upon one of the occasions that I was a visitor in Ko-tah's palace, I was passing through a little used corridor in going from one chamber to another, when just ahead of me a door opened and a man stepped out in front of me. When he heard my footsteps behind him he turned and looked at me, and then stepped quickly back into the apartment he had just left and closed the door hurriedly behind him. There would have been nothing particularly remarkable in that, had it not been for the fact that the man was not a Laythean, but unquestionably a Kalkar.

Believing that I had discovered an enemy in the very heart of Laythe, I leaped forward, and throwing open the door, followed into the apartment into which the man had disappeared. To my astonishment, I found myself confronted by six men, three of whom were Kalkars, while the other three were Laytheans, and among the latter I instantly recognized Ko-tah, himself. He flushed angrily as he saw me, but before he could speak I bowed and explained my action.

"I crave your pardon, Javadar," I said. "I thought that I saw an enemy of Laythe in the heart of your palace, and that by apprehending him I should serve you best;" and I started to withdraw from the chamber.

"Wait," he said. "You did right, but lest you misunderstand their presence here, I may tell you that these three are prisoners."

"I realized that at once when I saw you, Javadar," I replied, though I knew perfectly that he had lied to me; and then I backed from the room, closing the door after me.

I spoke to Moh-goh about it the next time that I saw him.

"You saw nothing, my friend," he said. "Remember that—you saw nothing."

"If you mean that it is none of my business, Moh-goh," I replied, "I perfectly agree with you, and you may rest assured that I shall not meddle in affairs that do not concern me."

However, I did considerable thinking upon the matter, and possibly I went out of my way a little more than one should who is attending strictly to his own business, that I might keep a little in touch with the course of the conspiracy, for no matter what I had said to Moh-goh, no matter how I attempted to convince myself that it did not interest me, the truth remained that anything that affected in any way the fate of Nah-ee-lah transcended in interest any event which might transpire within Va-nah, in so far as I was concerned.

The unobtrusive espionage which I practiced bore fruit, to the extent that it permitted me to know that on at least three other occasions delegations of Kalkars visited Ko-tah.

The fact that this ancient palace of the Prince of Laythe was a never-ending source of interest to me aided me in my self-imposed task of spying upon the conspirators, for the retainers of Ko-tah were quite accustomed to see me in out-of-the-way corridors and passages, oftentimes far from the inhabited portions of the building.

Upon the occasion of one of these tours I had descended to a lower terrace, along an ancient stone stairway which wound spirally downward and had discovered a dimly lighted room in which were stored a number of ancient works of art. I was quietly examining these, when I heard voices in an adjoining chamber.

"Upon no other conditions will he assist you, Javadar," said the speaker, whose voice I first heard.

"His demands are outrageous," replied a second speaker. "I refuse to consider them. Laythe is impregnable. He can never take it." The voice was that of Ko-tah.

"You do not know him, Laythean," replied the other. "He has given us engines of destruction with which we can destroy any city in Va-nah. He will give you Laythe. Is that not enough?"

"But he will be Jemadar of Jemadars and rule us all!" exclaimed Ko-tah. "The Jemadar of Laythe can be subservient to none."

"If you do not accede he will take Laythe in spite of you and reduce you to the status of a slave."

"Enough, Kalkar!" cried Ko-tah, his voice trembling with rage. "Be gone! Tell your master that Ko-tah refuses his base demands."

"You will regret it, Laythean," replied the Kalkar, "for you do not know what this creature has brought from another world in knowledge of war and the science of destruction of human life."

"I do not fear him," snapped Ko-tah, "my swords are many, my spearmen are well trained. Be gone, and do not return until your master is ready to sue with Ko-tah for an alliance."

I heard receding footsteps then, and following that, a silence which I thought indicated that all had left the chamber, but presently I heard Ko-tah's voice again.

"What think you of it?" he asked. And then I heard the voice of a third man, evidently a Laythean, replying:

"I think that if there is any truth in the fellow's assertions, we may not too quickly bring about the fall of Sagroth and place you upon the throne of Laythe, for only thus may we stand united against a common outside enemy."

"You are right," replied the Javadar. "Gather our forces. We shall strike within the ola."

I wanted to hear more, but they passed out of the chamber then, and their voices became only a subdued murmur which quickly trailed off into silence. What should I do? Within six hours Ko-tah would strike at the power of Sagroth, and I well knew what that would mean to Nah-ee-lah; either marriage with the new Jemadar, or death, and I guessed that the proud Princess would choose the latter in preference to Ko-tah.

Death Within and Without!

AS rapidly as I could I made my way from the palace of Ko-tah, and upward, terrace by terrace, toward the palace of the Jemadar. I had never presented myself at Sagroth's palace since Nah-ee-lah had so grievously offended me. I did not even know the customary procedure to follow to gain an audience with the Emperor, but nevertheless I came boldly to the carven gates and demanded to speak with the officer in command of the guards. When he came I told him that I desired to speak either with Sagroth or the Princess Nah-ee-lah at once, upon a matter of the most urgent importance.

"Wait," he said, "and I will take your message to the Jemadar."

He was gone for what seemed to me a very long time, but at last he returned, saying that Sagroth would see me at once, and I was conducted through the gates and into the palace toward the small audience chamber in which Sagroth had once received me so graciously. As I was ushered into the room I found myself facing both Sagroth and Nah-ee-lah. The attitude of the Jemadar seemed apparently judicial, but that of the Princess was openly hostile.

"What are you doing here, traitor?" she demanded, without waiting for Sagroth to speak, and at the same instant a door upon the opposite side of the room burst open and three warriors leaped into the apartment with bared swords. They wore the livery of Ko-tah, and I knew instantly the purpose for which they had come. Drawing my own sword, I leaped forward.

"I have come to defend the life of the Jemadar and his Princess," I cried, as I sprang between them and the advancing three.

"What means this?" demanded Sagroth. "How dare you enter the presence of your Jemadar with drawn sword?"

"They are the assassins of Ko-tah come to slay you!" I cried. "Defend yourself, Sagroth of Laythe!" And with that, I tried to engage the three until help arrived.

I am no novice with the sword. The art of fencing has been one of my chief diversions since my cadet days in the Air School, and I did not fear the Laytheans, though I knew that, even were they but mediocre swordsmen, I could not for long withstand the assaults of three at once. But upon this point I need not have concerned myself, for no sooner had I spoken than Sagroth's sword leaped from its scabbard, and placing himself at my side, he fought nobly and well in defense of his life and his honor.

The Moon Maid

One of our antagonists merely tried to engage me while the other two assassinated the Jemadar. And so, seeing that he was playing me, and that I could do with him about as I pleased if I did not push him too hard, I drove him back a few steps until I was close at the side of one of those who engaged Sagroth. Then before any could know my intention, I wheeled and lunged my sword through the heart of one of those who opposed the father of Nah-ee-lah. So quickly had I disengaged my former antagonist, so swift my lunge, that I had recovered and was ready to meet the renewed assaults of the first who had engaged me almost before he realized what had happened.

It was man against man, now, and the odds were even. I had no opportunity to watch Sagroth, but from the ring of steel on steel, I knew that the two were bitterly engaged. My own man kept me well occupied. He was a magnificent swordsman, but he was only fighting for his life; I was fighting for more—for my life and for my honor, too, since after the word "traitor" that Nah-ee-lah had hurled at me, I had felt that I must redeem myself in her eyes. I did not give any thought at all to the question as to just why I should care what Nah-ee-lah the Moon Maid thought of me, but something within me reacted mightily to the contempt that she had put into that single word.

I could catch an occasional glimpse of her standing there behind the massive desk at which her father had sat upon the first occasion of my coming to this chamber. She stood there very tense, her wide eyes fixed upon me in evident incredulity.

I had almost worn my man down and we were fighting now so that I was facing Nah-ee-lah, with my back toward the doorway through which the three assassins had entered. Sagroth must have been more than holding his own, too, for I could see his opponent slowly falling back before the older man's assaults. And then there broke above the clang of steel a girl's voice—Nah-ee-lah's—raised in accents of fear.

"Julian, beware! Behind you! Behind you!"

At the instant of her warning the eyes of my antagonist left mine, which, for his own good, they never should have done, and passed in a quick glance over my shoulder at something or someone behind me. His lack of concentration cost him his life. I saw my opening the instant that it was made, and with a quick lunge I passed my blade through his heart. Whipping it out again, I wheeled to face a dozen men springing into the chamber. They paid no attention to me, but leaped toward Sagroth, and before I could prevent it he went down with half a dozen blades through his body.

120

Upon the opposite side of the desk from us was another door-way directly behind Nah-ee-lah, and in the instant that she saw Sagroth fall, she called to me in a low voice: "Come, Julian, quick! Or we, too, are lost."

Realizing that the Jemadar was dead and that it would be folly to remain and attempt to fight this whole roomful of warriors, I leaped the desk and followed Nah-ee-lah through the doorway beyond. There was a cry, then, from someone within the room, to stop us, but Nah-ee-lah wheeled and slammed the door in their faces as they rushed forward, fastened it upon our side and then turned to me.

"Julian," she said, "how can you ever forgive me? You who have risked your life for the Jemadar, my father, in spite of the contemptible treatment that in my ignorance I have accorded you?"

"I could have explained," I said, "but you would not let me. Appearances were against me, and so I cannot blame you for thinking as you did."

"It was wicked of me not to listen to you, Julian, but I thought that Ko-tah had won you over, as he has won over even some of the staunchest friends of Sagroth."

"You might have known, Nah-ee-lah, that, even could I have been disloyal to your father, I never could have been disloyal to his daughter."

"I did not know," she said. "How could I?"

There suddenly came over me a great desire to take her in my arms and cover those lovely lips with kisses. I could not tell why this ridiculous obsession had seized upon me, nor why, of a sudden, I became afraid of little Nah-ee-lah, the Moon Maid. I must have looked very foolish indeed, standing there looking at her, and suddenly I realized how fatuous I must appear, and so I shook myself and laughed.

"Come, Nah-ee-lah," I said, "we must not remain here. Where can I take you, that you will be safe?"

"Upon the outer terrace there may be some of the loyal guards," she replied, "but if Ko-tah has already taken the palace, flight will be useless."

"From what I know of the conspiracy, it will be useless," I replied, "for the service of Sagroth and his palace is rotten with the spies and retainers of the Javadar."

"I feared as much," she said. "The very men who came to assassinate Sagroth wore the imperial livery less than an ola since."

"Are there none, then, loyal to you?" I asked her.

"The Jemadar's guard is always loyal," she said, "but they number scarce a thousand men."

"How may we summon them?" I asked.

"Let us go to the outer terraces and if there are any of them there we can congregate the balance, or as many of them as Ko-tah has left alive."

"Come, then," I said, "let us hasten;" and together, hand in hand, we ran along the corridors of the Jemadar's palace to the outer terraces of the highest tier of Laythe. There we found a hundred men, and when we had told them of what had happened within the palace they drew their swords and, surrounding Nah-ee-lah, they shouted:

"To the death for Nah-ee-lah, Jemadav of Laythe!"

They wanted to remain there and protect her, but I told them that there would be nothing gained by that, that sooner or later they would be overwhelmed by far greater numbers, and the cause of Nah-ee-lah lost.

"Send a dozen men," I said to their commander, "to rally all of the loyal guards that remain alive. Tell them to come to the throne room, ready to lay down their lives for the new Jemadav, and then let the dozen continue on out into the city, rallying the people to the protection of Nah-ee-lah. As for us, we will accompany her immediately to the throne room, and there, place her upon the throne and proclaim her ruler of Laythe. A hundred men may hold the throne room for a long time, if we reach it before Ko-tah reaches it with his forces."

The officer looked at Nah-ee-lah questioningly.

"Your command, Jemadav?" he inquired.

"We will follow the plan of Ju-lan the Javadar," she replied.

Immediately a dozen warriors were dispatched to rally the Imperial Guard and arouse the loyal citizens of the city to the protection of their new Jemadav, while the balance of us conducted Nah-ee-lah by a short course toward the throne room.

As we entered the great chamber at one end, Ko-tah and a handful of warriors came in at the other, but we had the advantage, in that we entered through a doorway directly behind the throne and upon the dais.

"Throw your men upon the main entrance," I called to the officer of the guard, "and hold it until reinforcements come," and then, as the hundred raced the length of the throne room toward the surprised and enraged Ko-tah, I led Nah-ee-lah to the central throne and seated her upon it. Then stepping forward, I raised my hand for silence.

"The Jemadar Sagroth is dead!" I cried. "Behold Nah-ee-lah, the Jemadav of Laythe!"

"Stop!" cried Ko-tah, "she may share the throne with me, but she may not possess it alone."

"Take that traitor!" I called to the loyal guard, and they rushed forward, evidently glad to do my bidding. But Ko-tah did not wait to be taken. He was accompanied by only a handful of men, and when he saw that the guard really intended to seize him and realized that he would be given short shrift at the hands of Nah-ee-lah and myself, he turned and fled. But I knew he would come back, and come back he did, though not until after the majority of the Jemadav's guard had gathered within the throne room.

He came with a great concourse of warriors, and the fighting was furious, but he might have brought a million men against our thousand and not immediately have overcome us, since only a limited number could fight at one time in the entrance way to the throne room. Already the corpses lay stacked as high as a man's head, yet no single member of Ko-tah's forces had crossed the threshold.

How long the fight was waged I do not know, but it must have been for a considerable time, since I know that our men fought in relays and rested many times, and that food was brought from other parts of the palace to the doorway behind the throne, and there were times when Ko-tah's forces withdrew and rested and recuperated, but always they came back in greater number, and eventually I realized we must be worn down by the persistence of their repeated attacks.

And then there arose slowly a deep-toned sound, at first we could not interpret. It rose and fell in increasing volume, until finally we knew that it was the sound of human voices, the voices of a great mob—of a mighty concourse of people and that it was sweeping toward us slowly and resistlessly.

Closer and closer it approached the palace as it rose, terrace upon terrace, toward the lofty pinnacle of Laythe. The fighting at the entrance to the throne room had almost ceased. Both sides were worn down almost to utter exhaustion, and now we but stood upon our arms upon either side of the wall of corpses that lay between us, our attention centered upon the sound of the growling multitude that was sweeping slowly upward toward us.

"They come," cried one of Nah-ee-lah's nobles, "to acclaim the new Jemadav and to tear the minions of Ko-tah the traitor to pieces!"

He spoke in a loud voice that was easily audible to Ko-tah and his retainers in the corridor without.

"They come to drag the spawn of Sagroth from the throne!" cried one of Ko-tah's followers. And then from the throne came the sweet, clear voice of Nah-ee-lah:

"Let the people's will be done," she said, and thus we stood, awaiting the verdict of the populace. Nor had we long to wait, for presently we realized that they had reached the palace terrace and entered the building itself. We could hear the shouting horde moving through the corridors and chambers, and finally the muffled bellowing resolved itself into articulate words:

"Sagroth is no more! Rule, Ko-tah, Jemadar of Laythe!"

I turned in consternation toward Nah-ee-lah. "What does it mean?" I cried. "Have the people turned against you?"

"Ko-tah's minions have done their work well during these many kelds," said the commander of the Jemadav's guard, who stood upon the upper steps of the dais, just below the throne. "They have spread lies and sedition among the people which not even Sagroth's just and kindly reign could overcome."

"Let the will of the people be done," repeated Nah-ee-lah.

"It is the will of fools betrayed by a scoundrel," cried the commander of the guard. "While there beats a single heart beneath the tunic of a guardsman of the Jemadav, we shall fight for Nah-ee-lah, Empress of Laythe."

Ko-tah's forces, now augmented by the rabble, were pushing their way over the corpses and into the throne room, so that we were forced to join the defenders, that we might hold them off while life remained to any of us. When the commander of the guard saw me fighting at his side he asked me to return to Nah-ee-lah.

"We must not leave the Jemadav alone," he said. "Return and remain at her side, Ju-lan the Javadar, and when the last of us has fallen, drive your dagger into her heart."

I shuddered and turned back toward Nah-ee-lah, The very thought of plunging my dagger into that tender bosom fairly nauseated me. "There must be some other way, and yet, what other means of escape could there be for Nah-ee-lah, who preferred death to the dishonor of surrender to Ko-tah, the murderer of her father? As I reached Nah-ee-lah's side, and turned again to face the entrance to the throne room, I saw that the warriors of Ko-tah were being pushed into the chamber by the mob behind them and that our defenders were being overwhelmed by the great number of their antagonists. Ko-tah, with a half dozen warriors, had been carried forward, practically without volition, by the press of numbers in their rear, and even now, with none to intercept him, was running rapidly up the broad center aisle toward the throne. Some of those in the entrance way saw him, and as he reached the foot of the steps leading to the dais, a snarling cry arose:

"Ko-tah the Jemadar!"

With bared sword, the fellow leaped toward me where I stood alone between Nah-ee-lah and her enemies.

"Surrender, Julian!" she cried. "It is futile to oppose them. You are not of Laythe. Neither duty nor honor impose upon you the necessity of offering your life for one of us. Spare him, Ko-tah!" she cried to the advancing Javadar, "and I will bow to the will of the people and relinquish the throne to you."

"Ko-tah the traitor shall never sit upon the throne of Nah-ee-lah!" I exclaimed, and leaping forward, I engaged the Prince of Laythe.

His warriors were close behind him, and it behooved me to work fast, and so I fought as I had never guessed that it lay within me to fight, and at the instant that the rabble broke through the remaining defenders and poured into the throne room of the Jemadars of Laythe, I slipped my point into the heart of Ko-tah. With a single piercing shriek, he threw his hands above his head and toppled backward down the steps to lie dead at the foot of the throne he had betrayed.

For an instant the silence of death reigned in the great chamber. Friend and foe stood alike in the momentary paralysis of shocked surprise.

That tense, breathless silence had endured for but a moment, when it was shattered by a terrific detonation. We felt the palace tremble and rock. The assembled mob looked wildly about, their eyes filled with fear and questioning. But before they could voice a question, another thunderous report burst upon our startled ears, and then from the city below the palace there arose the shrieks and screams of terrified people. Again the palace trembled, and a great crack opened in one of the walls of the throne room. The people saw it, and in an instant their anger against the dynasty of Sagroth was swallowed in the mortal terror which they felt for their own safety. With shrieks and screams they turned and bolted for the doorway. The weaker were knocked down and trampled upon. They fought with fists and swords and daggers, in their mad efforts to escape the crumbling building. They tore the clothing from one another, as each sought to drag back his fellow, that he might gain further in the race for the outer world.

And as the rabble fought, Nah-ee-lah and I stood before the throne of Laythe, watching them, while below us the few remaining members of the Jemadar's guard stood viewing in silent contempt the terror of the people.

Explosion after explosion followed one another in rapid succession. The people had fled. The palace was empty, except for that handful of us faithful ones who remained within the throne room.

"Let us go," I said to Nah-ee-lah, "and discover the origin of these sounds, and the extent of the damage that is being done."

"Come," she said, "here is a short corridor to the inner terrace, where we may look down upon the entire city of Laythe." And then, turning to the commander of the guard she said: "Proceed, please, to the palace gates, and secure them against the return of our enemies, if they have by this time all fled from the palace grounds."

The officer bowed, and followed by the few heroic survivors of the Jemadar's guard, he left by another corridor for the palace gates, while I followed Nah-ee-lah up a stairway that led to the roof of the palace.

Coming out upon the upper terrace, we made our way quickly to the edge overlooking the city and the crater. Below us a shrieking multitude ran hither and thither from terrace to terrace, while, now here and now there, terrific explosions occurred that shattered age-old structures and carried debris high into the air. Many terraces showed great gaps and tumbled ruins where other explosions had occurred and smoke and flames were rising from a dozen portions of the city.

But an instant it took me to realize that the explosions were caused by something that was being dropped into the city from above, and as I looked up I saw a missile describing an arc above the palace, past which it hurtled to a terrace far below, and at once I realized that the missile had originated outside the city. Turning quickly, I ran across the terrace to the outer side which overlooked the plateau upon which the city stood. I could not repress an exclamation of astonishment at the sight that greeted my eyes, for the surface of the plateau was alive with warriors. Nah-ee-lah had followed me and was standing at my elbow. "The Kalkars," she said. "They have come again to reduce Laythe. It has been long since they attempted it, many generations ago, but what is it, Julian, that causes the great noise and the destruction and the fires within Laythe?"

"It is this which fills me with surprise," I said, "and not the presence of the Kalkar warriors. Look! Nah-ee-lah," and I pointed to a knoll lying at the verge of the plateau, where, unless my eyes deceived me badly, there was mounted a mortar which was hurling shells into the city of Laythe. "And there, and there," I continued, pointing to other similar engines of destruction mounted at intervals. "The city is surrounded with them, Nah-ee-lah. Have your people any knowledge of such engines of warfare or of high explosives?" I demanded.

"Only in our legends are such things mentioned," she replied. "It has been ages since the inhabitants of Va-nah lost the art of manufacturing such things."

As we stood there talking, one of the Jemadar's guards emerged from the palace and approached us.

"Nah-ee-lah, Jemadav," he cried, "there is one here who craves audience with you and who says that if you listen to him you may save your city from destruction."

"Fetch him," replied Nah-ee-lah. "We will receive him here."

We had but a moment to wait when the guardsman returned with one of Ko-tah's captains.

"Nah-ee-lah, Jemadav," he cried, when she had given him permission to speak, "I come to you with a message from one who is Jemadar of Jemadars, ruler of all Va-nah. If you would save your city and your people, listen well."

The girl's eyes narrowed. "You are speaking to your Jemadav, fellow," she said. "Be careful, not only of your words, but of your tone,"

"I come but to save you," replied the man sullenly. "The Kalkars have discovered a great leader, and they have joined together from many cities to overthrow Laythe. My master does not wish to destroy this ancient city, and there is but one simple condition upon which he will spare it."

"Name your condition," said Nah-ee-lah.

"If you will wed him, he will make Laythe the capital of Va-nah, and you shall rule with him as Jemadav of Jemadavs."

Nah-ee-lah's lips curled in scorn. "And who is the presumptuous Kalkar that dares aspire to the hand of Nah-ee-lah?" she demanded.

"He is no Kalkar, Jemadav," replied the messenger. "He is one from another world, who says that he knows you well and that he has loved you long."

"His name," snapped Nah-ee-lah impatiently.

"He is called Or-tis, Jemadar of Jemadars."

Nah-ee-lah turned toward me with elevated brows and a smile of comprehension upon her face.

"Or-tis," she repeated.

"Now, I understand, my Jemadav," I said, "and I am commencing to have some slight conception of the time that must have elapsed since I first landed within Va-nah, for even since our escape from the Va-gas, Orthis has had time to discover the Kalkars and ingratiate himself among them, to conspire with them for the overthrow of Laythe, and to manufacture explosives and shells and the guns which are reducing Laythe this moment. Even had I not heard the name, I might have guessed that it was Orthis, for it is all so like him—ingrate, traitor, cur."

"Go back to your master," she said to the messenger, "and tell him that Nah-ee-lah, Jemadav of Laythe, would as leave mate with Ga-va-go the Va-ga as with him, and that Laythe will be happier destroyed and her people wiped from the face of Va-nah than ruled by such a beast. I have spoken. Go."

The fellow turned and left us, being accompanied from Nah-ee-lah's presence by the guardsman who had fetched him, and whom Nah-ee-lah commanded to return as soon as he had conducted the other outside the palace gates. Then the girl turned to me:

"O, Julian, what shall I do? How may I combat those terrible forces that you have brought to Va-nah from another world?"

I shook my head. "We, too, could manufacture both guns and ammunition to combat him, but now we have not the time, since Laythe will be reduced to a mass of ruins before we could even make a start. There is but one way, Nah-ee-lah, and that is to send your people—every fighting man that you can gather, and the women, too, if they can bear arms, out upon the plateau in an effort to overwhelm the Kalkars and destroy the guns."

She stood and thought for a long time, and presently the officer of the guard returned and halted before her, awaiting her commands. Slowly she raised her head and looked at him.

"Go into the city," she said, "and gather every Laythean who can carry a sword, a dagger, or a lance. Tell them to assemble on the inner terraces below the castle, and that I, Nah-ee-lah their Jemadav, will address them. The fate of Laythe rests with you. Go."

The Barsoom!

THE city was already in flames in many places, and though the people fought valiantly to extinguish them, it seemed to me that they but spread the more rapidly with each succeeding minute. And then, as suddenly as it had commenced, the bombardment ceased. Nah-ee-lah and I crossed over to the outer edge of the terrace to see if we could note any new movement by the enemy, nor did we have long to wait. We saw a hundred ladders raised as if by magic toward the lowest terrace, which rose but a bare two hundred feet above the base of the city. The men who carried the ladders were not visible to us when they came close to the base of the wall, but I guessed from the distant glimpses that I caught of the ladders as they were rushed forward by running men that here, again, Orthis' earthly knowledge and experience had come to the assistance of the Kalkars, for I was sure that only some form of extension ladder could be successfully used to reach even the lowest terrace.

When I saw their intention I ran quickly down into the palace and out upon the terrace before the gates, where the remainder of the guard were stationed, and there I told them what was happening and urged them to hasten the people to the lowest terrace to repulse the enemy before they had secured a foothold upon the city. Then I returned to Nah-ee-lah, and together we watched the outcome of the struggle, but almost from the first I realized that Laythe was doomed, for before any of her defenders could reach the spot, fully a thousand Kalkars had clambered to the terrace, and there they held their own while other thousands ascended in safety to the city.

We saw the defenders rush forth to attack them, and for a moment, so impetuous was their charge, I thought that I had been wrong and that the Kalkars might yet be driven from Laythe. Fighting upon the lower outer terrace far beneath us was a surging mass of shouting warriors. The Kalkars were falling back before the impetuous onslaught of the Laytheans.

"They have not the blood in their veins," whispered Nah-ee-lah, clinging tightly to my arm. "One noble is worth ten of them. Watch them. Already are they fleeing."

And so it seemed, and the rout of the Kalkars appeared almost assured, as score upon score of them were hurled over the edge of the terrace, to fall mangled and bleeding upon the ground hundreds of feet below.

But suddenly a new force seemed to be injected into the strife. I saw a stream of Kalkars emerging above the edge of the lower terrace—new men clambering up the ladders from the plateau below, and as they came they shouted something which I could not understand, but the other Kalkars seemed to take heart and made once more the semblance of a stand against the noble Laytheans, and I saw one, the leader of the newcomers, force his way into the battling throng. And then I saw him raise his hand above his head and hurl something into the midst of the compact ranks of the Laytheans.

Instantly there was a terrific explosion and a great, bloody gap lay upon the terrace where an instant before a hundred of the flower of the fighting men of Laythe had been so gloriously defending their city and their honor.

"Grenades," I exclaimed. "Hand grenades!"

"What is it, Julian? What is it that they are doing down there?" cried Nah-ee-lah. "They are murdering my people."

"Yes, Nah-ee-lah, they are murdering your people, and well may Va-nah curse the day that Earth Men set foot upon your world."

"I do not understand, Julian," she said.

"This is the work of Orthis," I said, "who has brought from Earth the knowledge of diabolical engines of destruction. He first shelled the city with what must have been nothing more than crude mortars, for it is impossible that he has had the time to construct the machinery to build any but the simplest of guns. Now his troops are hurling hand grenades among your men. There is no chance, Nah-ee-lah, for the Laytheans to successfully pit their primitive weapons against the modern agents of destruction which Orthis has brought to bear against them. Laythe must surrender or be destroyed."

Nah-ee-lah laid her head upon my shoulder and wept softly. "Julian," she said at last, "this is the end, then. Take me to the Jemadav, my mother, please, and then you must go and make your peace with your fellow Earth Man. It is not right that you, a stranger, who have done so much for me, should fall with me and Laythe."

"The only peace I can make with Orthis, Nah-ee-lah," I replied, "is the peace of death. Orthis and I may not live together again in the same world."

She was crying very softly, sobbing upon my shoulder, and I put my arm about her in an effort to quiet her.

"I have brought you only suffering and danger, and now death, Julian," she said, "when you deserve naught but happiness and peace."

I suddenly felt very strange and my heart behaved wretchedly, so that when I attempted to speak it pounded so that I could say nothing and my knees shook beneath me. What had come over me? Could it be possible that already Orthis had loosed his poison gas? Then, at last, I managed to gather myself together.

"Nah-ee-lah," I said, "I do not fear death if you must die, and I do not seek happiness except with you."

She looked up suddenly, her great, tear-dimmed eyes wide and gazing deep into mine.

"You mean—Julian? You mean—?"

"I mean, Nah-ee-lah, that I love you," I replied, though I must have stumbled through the words in a most ridiculous manner, so frightened was I.

"Ah, Julian," she sighed, and put her arms about my neck.

"And you, Nah-ee-lah!" I exclaimed incredulously, as I crushed her to me, "can it be that you return my love?"

"I have loved you always," she replied. "From the very first, almost —way back when we were prisoners together in the No-vans' village. You Earth Men must be very blind, my Julian. A Laythean would have known it at once, for it seemed to me that upon a dozen occasions I almost avowed my love openly to you."

"Alas, Nah-ee-lah! I must have been very blind, for I had not guessed until this minute that you loved me."

"Now," she said, "I do not care what happens. We have one another, and if we die together, doubtless we shall live together in a new incarnation."

"I hope so," I said, "but I should much rather be sure of it and live together in this."

"And I, too, Julian, but that is impossible."

We were walking now through the corridors of the palace toward the chamber occupied by her mother, but we did not find her there and Nah-ee-lah became apprehensive as to her safety. Hurriedly we searched through other chambers of the palace, until at last we came to the little audience chamber in which Sagroth had been slain, and as we threw open the door I saw a sight that I tried to hide from Nah-ee-lah's eyes as I drew her around in an effort to force her back into the corridor. Possibly she guessed what impelled my action, for she shook her head and murmured: "No, Julian; whatever it is I must see it." And then she pushed her way gently past me, and we stood together upon the threshold, looking at the harrowing sight which the interior of the room displayed.

There were the bodies of the assassins Sagroth and I had slain, and the dead Jemadar, too, precisely as he had fallen, while across his breast lay the body of Nah-ee-lah's mother, a dagger self-thrust through her heart. For just a moment Nah-ee-lah stood there looking at them in silence, as though in prayer, and then she turned wearily away and left the chamber, closing the door behind her. We walked on in silence for some time, ascending the stairway back to the upper terrace. Upon the inner side, the flames were spreading throughout the city, roaring like a mighty furnace and vomiting up great clouds of smoke, for though the Laythean terraces are supported by tremendous arches of masonry, yet there is much wood used in the interior construction of the buildings, while the hangings and the furniture are all inflammable.

"We had no chance to save the city," said Nah-ee-lah, with a sigh. "Our people, called from their normal duties by the false Ko-tah, were leaderless. The fire fighters, instead of being at their posts, were seeking the life of their Jemadar. Unhappy day! Unhappy day!"

"You think they could have stopped the fire?" I asked.

"The little ponds, the rivulets, the waterfalls, the great public baths and the tiny lakes that you see upon every terrace were all built with fire protection in mind. It is easy to divert their waters and flood any tier of buildings. Had my people been at their posts, this, at least, could not have happened."

As we stood watching the flames we suddenly saw people emerging in great numbers upon several of the lower terraces. They were evidently in terrified flight, and then others appeared upon terraces above them—Kalkars who hurled hand grenades amongst the Laytheans beneath them. Men, women, and children ran hither and thither, shrieking and crying and seeking for shelter, but from the buildings behind them, rushing them outward upon the terraces, came other Kalkars with hand grenades. The fires hemmed the people of Laythe upon either side and the Kalkars attacked them from the rear and from above. The weaker fell and were trodden to death, and I saw scores fall upon their own lances or drive daggers into the hearts of their loved ones.

The massacre spread rapidly around the circumference of the city and the Kalkars drove the people from the upper terraces downward between the raging fires which were increasing until the mouth of the great crater was filled with roaring flames and smoke. In the occasional gaps we could catch glimpses of the holocaust beneath us.

A sudden current of air rising from the crater lifted the smoke pall high for a moment, revealing the entire circumference of the crater, the edge of which was crowded with Laytheans. And then I saw a warrior from the opposite side leap upon the surrounding wall that bordered the lower terrace at the edge of the yawning crater. He turned and called aloud some message to his fellows, and then wheeling, threw his arms above his head and leaped outward into the yawning, bottomless abyss. Instantly the others seemed to be inoculated with the infection of his mad act. A dozen men leaped to the wall and dove head foremost into the crater. The thing spread slowly at first, and then with the rapidity of a prairie fire, it ran around the entire circle of the city. Women hurled their children in and then leaped after them. The multitude fought one with another for a place upon the wall from which they might cast themselves to death. It was a terrible—an awe-inspiring sight.

Nah-ee-lah covered her eyes with her hands. "My poor people!" she cried. "My poor people!" And far below her, by the thousands now, they were hurling themselves into eternity, while above them the screaming Kalkars hurled hand grenades among them and drove the remaining inhabitants of Laythe, terrace by terrace, down toward the crater's rim.

Nah-ee-lah turned away. "Come, Julian," she said, "I cannot look, I cannot look." And together we walked across the terrace to the outer side of the city.

Almost directly beneath us upon the next terrace was a palace gate and as we reached a point where we could see it, I was horrified to see that the Kalkars had made their way up the outer terraces to the very palace walls. The Jemadar's guard was standing there ready to defend the palace against the invaders. The great stone gates would have held indefinitely against spears and swords, but even the guardsmen must have guessed that their doom was already sealed and that these gates, that had stood for ages, an ample protection to the Jemadars of Laythe, were about to fall, as the Kalkars halted fifty yards away, and from their ranks a single individual stepped forth a few paces.

As my eyes alighted upon him I seized Nah-ee-lah's arm. "Orthis!" I cried. "It is Orthis." At the same instant the man's eyes rose above the gates and fell upon us. A nasty leer curled his lips as he recognized us.

"I come to claim my bride," he cried, in a voice that reached us easily, "and to balance my account with you, at last," and he pointed a finger at me.

In his right hand he held a large, cylindrical object, and as he ceased speaking he hurled it at the gates precisely as a baseball pitcher pitches a swift ball.

The missile struck squarely at the bottom of the gates. There was a terrific explosion, and the great stone portals crumbled, shattered into a thousand fragments. The last defense of the Empress of Laythe had fallen, and with it there went down in bloody death at least half the remaining members of her loyal guard.

Instantly the Kalkars rushed forward, hurling hand grenades among the survivors of the guard.

Nah-ee-lah turned toward me and put her arms about my neck.

"Kiss me once more, Julian," she said, "and then the dagger."

"Never, never, Nah-ee-lah!" I cried. "I cannot do it."

"But I can!" she exclaimed, and drew her own from its sheath at her hip.

I seized her wrist. "Not that, Nah-ee-lah!" I cried. "There must be some other way." And then there came to me a mad inspiration. "The wings!" I cried. "Where are they kept? The last of your people have been destroyed. Duty no longer holds you here. Let us escape, even if it is only to frustrate Orthis' plans and deny him the satisfaction of witnessing our death."

"But, where can we go?" she asked.

"We may at least choose our own manner of death," I replied, "far from Laythe and far from the eyes of an enemy who would gloat over our undoing."

"You are right, Julian. We still have a little time, for I doubt if Orthis or his Kalkars can quickly find the stairway leading to this terrace." And then she led me quickly to one of the many towers that rise above the palace. Entering it, we ascended a spiral staircase to a large chamber at the summit of the tower. Here were kept the imperial wings. I fastened Nah-ee-lah's to her and she helped me with mine, and then from the pinnacle of the tower we arose above the burning city of Laythe and flew rapidly toward the distant lowlands and the sea. It was in my mind to search out, if possible, the location of the Barsoom, for I still entertained the mad hope that my companions yet lived—if I did, why not they?

The heat above the city was almost unendurable and the smoke suffocating, yet we passed through it, so that almost immediately we were hidden from the view of that portion of the palace from which we had arisen, with the result that when Orthis and his Kalkars finally found their way to the upper terrace, as I have no doubt they did, we had disappeared—whither they could not know.

We flew and drifted with the wind across the mountainous country toward the plains and the sea, it being my intention upon reaching the latter to follow the coast line until I came to a river marked by an island at its mouth. From that point I knew that I could reach the spot where the Barsoom had landed.

Our long flight must have covered a considerable period of time, since it was necessary for us to alight and rest many times and to search for food. We met, fortunately, with no mishaps, and upon the several occasions when we were discovered by roving bands of Va-gas we were able to soar far aloft and escape them easily. We came at length, however, to the sea, the coast of which I followed to the left, but though we passed the mouths of many rivers, I discovered none that precisely answered the description of that which I sought.

It was borne in upon me at last that our quest was futile, but where we were to find a haven of safety neither of us could guess. The gas in our bags was losing its buoyancy and we had no means wherewith to replenish it. It would still maintain us for a short time, but how long neither of us knew, other than that it had not nearly the buoyancy that it originally possessed.

Off the coast we had seen islands almost continuously and I suggested to Nah-ee-lah that we try to discover one upon which grew the fruits and nuts and vegetables necessary for our subsistence, and where we might also have a constant supply of fresh water.

I discovered that Nah-ee-lah knew little about these islands, practically nothing in fact, not even as to whether they were inhabited; but we determined to explore one, and to this end we selected an island of considerable extent that lay about ten miles off shore. We reached it without difficulty and circled slowly above it, scrutinizing its entire area carefully. About half of it was quite hilly, but the balance was rolling and comparatively level. We discovered three streams and two small lakes upon it, and an almost riotous profusion of vegetable growth, but nowhere did we discern the slightest indication that it was inhabited. And so at last, feeling secure, we made our landing upon the plain, close to the beach.

It was a beautiful spot, a veritable Garden of Eden, where we two might have passed the remainder of our lives in peace and security, for though we later explored it carefully, we found not the slightest evidence that it had ever known the foot of man.

Together we built a snug shelter against the storms. Together we hunted for food, and during our long periods of idleness we lay upon the soft sward beside the beach, and to pass the time away, I taught Nah-ee-lah my own language.

It was a lazy, indolent, happy life that we spent upon this enchanted isle, and yet, though we were happy in our love, each of us felt the futility of our existence, where our lives must be spent in useless idleness.

We had, however, given up definitely hope for any other form of existence. And thus we were lying one time, as was our wont after eating, stretched in luxurious ease upon our backs on the soft lunar grasses, I with my eyes closed, when Nah-ee-lah suddenly grasped me by the arm.

"Julian," she cried, "what is it? Look!"

I opened my eyes, to find her sitting up and gazing into the sky toward the mainland, a slim forefinger indicating the direction of the object that had attracted her attention and aroused her surprised interest.

The Moon Maid

As my eyes rested upon the thing her pointing finger indicated, I leaped to my feet with an exclamation of incredulity, for there, sailing parallel with the coast at an altitude of not more than a thousand feet, was a ship, the lines of which I knew as I had known my mother's face. It was the Barsoom.

Grasping Nah-ee-lah by the arm, I dragged her to her feet. "Come, quick, Nah-ee-lah!" I cried, and urged her rapidly toward our hut, where we had stored the wings and the gas bags which we had never thought to use again, yet protected carefully, though why we knew not.

There was still gas in the bags—enough to support us in the air, with the assistance of our wings, but to fly thus for long distances would have been most fatiguing, and there was even a question as to whether we could cross the ten miles of sea that lay between us and the mainland; yet I was determined to attempt it. Hastily we donned the wings and bags, and rising together, flapped slowly in the direction of the mainland.

The Barsoom was cruising slowly along a line that would cross ours before we could reach the shore, but I hoped that they would sight us and investigate.

We flew as rapidly as I dared, for I could take no chances upon exhausting Nah-ee-lah, knowing that it would be absolutely impossible for me to support her weight and my own, with our depleted gas bags. There was no way in which I could signal to the Barsoom. We must simply fly toward her. That was the best that we could do, and finally, try though we would, I realized that we should be too late to intercept her and that unless they saw us and changed their course, we should not come close enough to hail them. To see my friends passing so near, and yet to be unable to apprise them of my presence filled me with melancholy. Not one of the many vicissitudes and dangers through which I had passed since I left Earth depressed me more than the sight of the Barsoom forging slowly past us without speaking. I saw her change her course then and move inland still further from us, and I could not but dwell upon our unhappy condition, since now we might never again be able to reach the safety of our island, there being even a question as to whether the gas bags would support us to the mainland.

They did, however, and there we alighted and rested, while the Barsoom sailed out of sight toward the mountains.

"I shall not give it up, Nah-ee-lah," I cried. "I am going to follow the Barsoom until we find it, or until we die in the attempt. I doubt if we ever can reach the island again, but we can make short flights here on land, and by so doing, we may overtake my ship and my companions."

After resting for a short time, we arose again, and when we were above the trees I saw the Barsoom far in the distance, and again it was circling, this time toward the left, so we altered our course and flew after it. But presently we realized that it was making a great circle and hope renewed within our breasts, giving us the strength to fly on and on, though we were forced to come down often for brief rests. As we neared the ship we saw that the circles were growing smaller, but it was not until we were within about three miles of her that I realized that she was circling the mouth of a great crater, the walls of which rose several hundred feet above the surrounding country. We had been forced to land again to rest, when there flashed upon my mind a sudden realization of the purpose of the maneuvers of the Barsoom—she was investigating the crater, preparatory to an attempt to pass through it into outer space and seek to return to Earth again.

As this thought impinged upon my brain, a wave of almost hopeless horror overwhelmed me as I thought of being definitely left forever by my companions and that by but a few brief minutes. Nah-ee-lah was to be robbed of life and happiness and peace, for at that instant the hull of the Barsoom dropped beneath the rim of the crater and disappeared from our view.

Rising quickly with Nah-ee-lah, I flew as rapidly as my tired muscles and exhausted gas bag would permit toward the rim of the crater. In my heart of hearts I knew that I should be too late, for once they had decided to make the attempt, the ship would drop like a plummet into the depths, and by the time I reached the mouth of the abyss it would be lost to my view forever.

And yet I struggled on, my lungs almost bursting from the exertion of my mad efforts toward speed. Nah-ee-lah trailed far behind, for if either of us could reach the Barsoom in time we should both be saved, and I could fly faster than Nah-ee-lah; otherwise, I should never have separated myself from her by so much as a hundred yards.

Though my lungs were pumping like bellows, I venture to say that my heart stood still for several seconds before I topped the crater's rim.

At the same instant that I expected the last vestige of my hopes to be dashed to pieces irrevocably and forever, I crossed the rim and beheld the Barsoom not twenty feet below me, just over the edge of the abyss, and upon her deck stood West and Jay and Norton.

As I came into view directly above them, West whipped out his revolver and leveled it at me, but the instant that his finger pressed the trigger Norton sprang forward and struck his hand aside.

"My God, sir!" I heard the boy cry, "it is the Captain." And then they all recognized me, and an instant later I almost collapsed as I fell to the deck of my beloved ship.

My first thought was of Nah-ee-lah, and at my direction the Barsoom rose swiftly and moved to meet her.

*

"Great Scott!" cried my guest, leaping to his feet and looking out of the stateroom window, "I had no idea that I had kept you up all night. Here we are in Paris already."

"But the rest of your story," I cried. "You have not finished it, I know. Last night, as you were watching them celebrating in the Blue Room, you made a remark which led me to believe that some terrible calamity threatened the world."

"It does," he said, "and that was what I meant to tell you about, but this story of the third incarnation of which I am conscious was necessary to an understanding of how the great catastrophe overwhelmed the people of the earth."

"But, did you reach Earth again?" I demanded.

"Yes," he said, "in the year 2036. I had been ten years within Va-nah, but did not know whether it was ten months or a century until we landed upon Earth."

He smiled then. "You notice that I still say I. It is sometimes difficult for me to recall which incarnation I am in. Perhaps it will be clearer to you if I say Julian 5th returned to Earth in 2036, and in the same year his son, Julian 6th, was born to his wife, Nah-ee-lah the Moon Maid."

"But how could he return to Earth in the disabled Barsoom?"

"Ah," he said, "that raises a point that was of great interest to Julian 5th. After he regained the Barsoom, naturally one of the first questions he asked was as to the condition of the ship and their intentions, and when he learned that they had, in reality, been intending to pass through the crater toward the Earth he questioned them further and discovered that it was the young ensign, Norton, who had repaired the engine, having been able to do it by information that he had gleaned from Orthis, after winning the latter's friendship. Thus was explained the intimacy between the two, which Julian 5th had so deplored, but which he now saw that young Norton had encouraged for a patriotic purpose."

"We are docked now and I must be going. Thank you for your hospitality and for your generous interest," and he held out his hand toward me.

"But the story of Julian 9th," I insisted, "am I never to hear that?"

"If we meet again, yes," he promised, with a smile.

"I shall hold you to it," I told him.

"If we meet again," he repeated, and departed, closing the stateroom door after him.

—

www.ingramcontent.com/pod-product-compliance
Lightning Source LLC
Chambersburg PA
CBHW051846170626
46807CB00003B/1375